Sod
the
bitches!

Sod the bitches!

STEVEN BERKOFF

URBANE Publications

urbanepublications.com

First published in Great Britain in 2015
by Urbane Publications Ltd
Suite 3, Brown Europe House, 33/34 Gleamingwood Drive, Chatham,
Kent ME5 8RZ

Copyright © Steven Berkoff, 2015

The moral right of Steven Berkoff to be identified as the author of this work has been asserted in accordance with the Copyright, Designs and Patents Act of 1988.

All rights reserved. No part of this publication may be reproduced, stored in a retrieval system, or transmitted in any form or by any means, electronic, mechanical, photocopying, recording or otherwise, without the prior permission of both the copyright owner and the above publisher of this book. This book is a work of fiction. Names, characters, places, organisations and incidents either are products of the author's imagination or are used fictitiously. Apart from historical fact, any resemblance to actual events, organisations, or persons living or dead, is entirely coincidental
A CIP catalogue record for this book is available
from the British Library.

ISBN 978-1-909273-82-5

Design and Typeset by Julie Martin
Cover design by Julie Martin

Printed in Great Britain by
CPI Group (UK) Ltd,
Croydon, CR0 4YY

URBANE
Publications

urbanepublications.com

FSC

The publisher supports the Forest Stewardship Council® (FSC®), the leading international forest-certification organisation. This book is made from acid-free paper from an FSC®-certified provider. FSC is the only forest-certification scheme supported by the leading environmental organisations, including Greenpeace.

FOR CLARA

PROLOGUE

The Bitches!

Bloody bitches! Fuck the lot of them, grubby slags writing their cheap reviews as if their lives depended on it ... second string scum, hoping to impress their bosses with how scathing, catty, vicious and nasty they can be with their unfettered bile ... cold beasts, dead souls, not knowing how hard it is for a man to sweat his guts out on a stage. How hard, each night to go through what he has to go through, through rain or shine, pain, mental confusion, emotional wounds ... but still get out there and do it while they just drop their fat arse in a seat and work on their lazy vitriol.

Where did they learn such loathsome nastiness? At university I expect where smart, snooty-arsed cynicism is the order of the day. They grovel around for three years, get some half-baked degree and then write swinish arse-licking letters to some slob-bollocks at one of the 'quality' papers, working their way down until they get in as a second-stringer to some drunken overlord and fill in on his hungover days off. Then ... Eureka! ... they're given a chance at reviewing the codswallop fringe 'smart theatre', one of those atrocious, shitty revivals of Pinter or Beckett, directed by a hipster-faced lying runt who has never been exposed for the moronic dope he is because the critics seem to be on moron-nodding terms – they believe that if they've suffered for three hours it must be bloody good.

So against the backdrop sludgeheap of slime, yours truly has to wend his weary way, manfully attempting to embolden the works of Shakespeare, Shaw or Sheridan, hauling it up out of the slimy morass of dry-ice machines and taped crap sound-effects. Drag it out, coated in filth and slime from years of 'creative' abuse, clean it up painstakingly, then train yourself to be pure, committed, inventive, loving and embrace the play with all the passion you can summon. Then you present it – alive, daringly fresh, sharp, *audible* – and some posh little bitch, rotting from years of self-indulgent self-abuse and self-centredness doesn't recognise this vibrant piece of theatrical energy in front of her, can't see the dynamic beast before her very eyes, since she's so acclimatised to the fat, rich wanker's shit that coats all productions, so acclimatised to the smell of his rotting cankered junk-producing brain, that she feels she's missing something in the performance.

Where is that familiar stench of poo she inwardly squeals ... she panics, or is

SO TOTALLY BORED!!

Oh yes, we've heard that one before. But now she goes away to make her own shit, her own damnable excrescence. And she feels happy again ... oh so happy!

Now why had it come to this? Why, now, does our poor player feel the bitches are out to get him? Since these feelings must have developed from somewhere. Why in recent years has he noticed they can be far more vicious than men (some men that is)? Is it that the fairer sex have become contaminated in some way by the eons of abuse from men? Or is it that their focus on life is narrower, smaller, more precisely hardwired to relate only to what directly concerns them? Do they therefore lack an overview, a more cosmological concept of the world? Or is that just more abuse from men? Or a man in this instance. Yes, they can be more detailed, analytical about what directly impinges upon their own hormonal needs and desires. And something socially and artistically out of their narrow beam of interest cannot be related to, or understood.

Out of focus so to speak, like a camera with a lens that brings what is directly in front of it into sharp focus, but leaves the rest of the world as a strange indecipherable blur.

At least this excuses them somewhat. Somewhat. Even when celebs are being interviewed by a woman it always and steadily focuses on the celeb's love life, his cocksman status, his past iniquities, when I am hungry to learn how he prepared to play Macbeth or Shylock. We always go down the same weary, puddled path to slush and slime, since this is the path most compelling to the hag, and in that case why should there be bitch critics at all? Hmmm ... a thought to ponder upon.

CHAPTER 1

Tea, theatre, life

A thought to ponder indeed. I broke off from this whining stream of pissy philosophy and put the kettle on for the umpteenth time. The kettle boils. Grey clouds perpetually graze past the window. It's a typical drab London day and you notice it all the more when the days are somewhat vacant, and somehow waiting for the nights makes the days seem all the more defunct by contrast so I'll have to get down to the gym; which would be nice if I didn't hate it so much.

There is a SHE in the house and has been in the house for some time and while we get on well together the fires have long ago faded, if not quite gone out, and that may even be the reason why we do get on, since what we have in common is far more than JUST that. However, when the chemicals in the body rage we have both exploited opportunities to take the horse for a canter so to speak, and slake the beast's thirst. You can lead a horse to water, and it's good to let him drink. In the past these could get quite intense and complicated even in their most exhilarating effervescence. Sometimes the women actually thought that I'd break up my marriage for them. No, no, not a hope in hell, although there were some painful and nerve-shattering repercussions and breakdowns on my part, but she nursed me through it since we were partners.

AFTER ALL.

I drank my green tea and stared out of the window and it all looked utterly dreary except when the weather broke, and spring plumped the trees up with bright green and the cat sat on the wall. Then the house could be a nice welcoming old Victorian pile. It was on the verges of Islington which had pleasantly yuppified itself over the last twenty or so years, gaining a lot whilst it also lost its wonderful old idiosyncratic character. Its antique market is a sliver of what it once was, and the ghastly cancer of commerce has invaded, the vile stores metastasising and slowly strangling all else out. But it still had the remnants of sauce and the smell and the old boys and girls were still there, hanging on by their nails while the thieving landlords kept increasing the rent. The beautiful working-man's café on the corner of the green formerly known as Alfredo's, an indomitable church of working-class junk food with occasional fabulous treats, had now gone — but replaced by an equally good pseudo working-class eatery so that wasn't such a bad swap.

Other sublime treasures have crumbled to dust.

Within the antique market there used to be a wonderful faux Victorian café run by a couple of queers who had that intrinsic sense of style queers have, making the place a warm sanctuary of pots of tea and crumbling toasted cheese sandwiches against a background of thirties music. Yes, it was mumsyish! Your very existence was improved by resting there for an hour. Oh how I miss you all! And there was such a charming cockney pooftah who dealt in shabby bits of art deco and who did the most sublime impersonation of Marlene Dietrich, and when he did you swore you saw that bizarre and exotic lady right there in front of you.

These were the people of the city, of the markets, and the market was our bolthole where we would gather every Wednesday and Saturday, and sit in the cafés and chatter. Now the nice cafés have gone. Sadly.

However, a small theatre was left in the area where they paid you hardly anything and you happily worked for the glory of it, a stinking hell hole of a place with one smelly dressing room at the back for both sexes. But it was the place to work if you were on your back legs and nothing much was coming in and there was an opportunity to do some acting.

Oh you might feel shabby going back there if you had originally advanced from there, if that was one of your launching pads to future exotic worlds and you entered the real tumbling dynamic world of the West End in a small or mini hit, and you got to know the actors in the other theatres, and a real run was when the seasons changed in front of you, and winter became spring, and still you were doing your six, seven or even, if unlucky, eight shows a week. To do the same play night after night you need the patience of a gladiator and the guts of an accountant! Reverse that.

It becomes brutal after the first six or so weeks, and after that just crawling into your dressing room can be a glimmer of hell, but when it's over the hell suddenly morphs into heaven. I have never known any activity where there's such a complete reversal of mood.

I was getting ready for the little pub in Islington where the lovely anglophile American presides over the shabby, squalid but exquisite tiny theatre, sometime pulling the pints and sometimes directing the plays.

I waited opposite, just waited by the church opposite the theatre until the last minute, the last few minutes when they called the 'five' and then slinked in hoping not to see any 'friends' who might stop me and cry out … "Oh we're coming to see you tonight"… which was the last thing I wanted to hear just before going on. So I slunk in like a criminal who has just committed a sordid crime and is slinking away trying to make himself invisible. It was that or having to go in early at the half and hear the drab bric-a-brac chatter of the actors, their grungy stories and idle gossip, and that could make me even more unsettled. But hey, it was summer and I could always nip out to the tiny courtyard and roll a fag for a final puff.

But I waited, and then at five to eight I crossed the road and slipped in, swiftly changed and was ready.

Ready and able and had the part under my belt. "We've got clearance!" the stage manager said and we drifted on like ghosts and took our places.

The lights exploded on to the stage and the music slammed in and all was highly organised chaos. It was a bar in some faded old hotel. The lines began, the characters told their stories and the laughter came thick and furious and at the end the audience cheered and so it was good, and I felt good, and the cast felt good, and we drank in the pub bar and the friends who came said it was good, and everyone was chuffed and feeling really good that we had got through another night.

CHAPTER 2

I live the performance

And yes it was good. That's all you need. Your worth has been proved. What you waited for all day, what you had prepared for, saved yourself for, had been accomplished and you were allowed to live for yet one more day ... a reprieve for one more day until you would have to prove yourself yet again. But for now you had earned your freedom and could have your first drink and that was always the best one. The first one after the show. The sacrifice when you had earned the right to live for another day.

If it was a warm night we might spill out onto the pavement and lose the stinking fetid pub smell of sour beer. Everybody reacts in their own way which is quite natural but some just can't give you any praise or warmth and feel tight-arsed about even saying they enjoyed it; and if they didn't, and didn't wish to think of themselves as hypocrites, would say:

I live the performance

"How do you think it went tonight?"

How do *I* think it went?! And you want to say:

"How should *I* fucking know, I wasn't out there in the audience you cunt. You were!"

But instead, knowing they're arseholes and many are like them, just reply, "It felt great and the audience responded really well".

And then you drift off to a kinder spot and a smiling mouth and a bit of response since secretly that's what all actors need even if they might give the opposite impression.

A good night would be when a friend dropped by, preferably a young sexy woman friend, and you'd slip off for a meal somewhere, maybe the Turkish just round the corner where it was snug and cosy, and warm-hearted. And if it was summer then you'd sit outside and order some humus and tahini plus some stuffed vine leaves and aubergine dip and some 'delish' red wine, sipping it slowly, feeling the gorgeous blood-red juice refill your veins that had bled themselves for the performance, since that's how it feels when you've given your all, that's really how it feels ... like a bloodletting.

Yes, for sure, like stepping into the ring. But each night, and no matter what you fear, and the greatest fear is losing the words, somehow your brain holds onto the words with the ferocity of a wolf protecting her cubs since the brain knows which part is the guardian of the words, knows that without the words you die, and so the brain holds on to the words even if you have slivers of fear cutting through you like icy blades.

And sometimes the fear was terrible, just absolutely terrible, for whatever reason. Who was to know? Who knew why you were full of confidence one night and shaking like a leaf the next. But the nights when you were full of fear you did the most terrible thing an actor can do and that is anticipate your next line ... run it through silently in your head to make sure before you get there and that is the most terrible thing to do since you are no longer on automatic. You have switched to manual ... oooh!

Best keep the mind clear, just listen to what the other actors are saying and doing and let it pop out automatically... then it's wonderful and free and you can colour the text, invest it with all sorts of sounds and images. Then it's good and you're cool and you fly along and it gets exciting. And somehow the audience can feel when you're flying and abandoned, and they like that, in fact they love it when you're flying and abandoned cause they sense that you are unpredictable and can't guess what you are going to do next, and those are the nights I love the best. When I am outrageous, daring, dangerous, but still totally within the character – not betraying the character but

LIBERATING IT.

Now I have a reprieve for one more night, just until the

next night, and soon it will be over, the agony of pain and pleasure, fear and exaltation, and like all actors I look forward to the end, and yes, miss it when its gone and wish for the cycle of pain and pleasure all over again, like a strung-out junkie.

But now I'm sipping the wine and chatting to my lover and that feels so nice. So very nice since my wife's away ... oh joy! Sometimes she does go away, even for a few days, since her work might take her out of London, as she's a specialised nurse and is often asked for when an old client falls ill and just wants her there for even a few days.

And so now this is one of those times and though I love my wife dearly and would never consider leaving her, I also have to function as a male and I adore the occasional fuck. In fact could not live without the occasional

FUCK.

And what a sweet reward when after a performance I am free to see my favourite lover and know that at the end of the evening I will be inside her, right inside, and oh how good is that ... how wonderful is that!

And sometimes in bed when I am grinding my performance into her and she is smiling and squirming she is apt to say "Who do you love best?" and I say that my love for you darling is quite different from my love for her, since I do love her, she has been my wife for many years, and that is a different kind of love than the one I have for you which is thrilling, thrilling beyond compare. And what a sweet body hath she, how lyrical, svelte, lithesome and young, how lovely she is, how fondant, pretty and so horny. But like so many women, ever so slightly barmy, so I have to be careful.

Mate! I know you hear me.

I try to be truthful as much as I can, and not lie for a fuck but not stint her either of the huge affection I feel for her, really huge, abandoned. And it will grow even huger when she threatens to leave me, when she threatens to leave me unless I abandon my wife and move in with her. Ah, then the love miraculously grows. Oh how it grows when there is a threat under it, oh how you value what you may lose, value like there is nothing on earth like her. My cock runneth over. That's poetry.

"Fuck me darling as hard as you can, fuck me hard darling", and I did, yes I did … within the limits of a middle aged lothario that is.

Her breath as she sleeps just brushes my face and is the sweetest thing on earth.

--- --- ---

CHAPTER 3

Poached eggs and puddings

I crawled up the road to the café for breakfast since that's what I do when my missus isn't there as we always have breakfast together and it's nice and comforting and sometimes boring. But when she's not there then I crawl up the road to the Italian greasy spoon and I am always greeted with such affection by the Mama who runs the café with her son, and while the mum is Italian, the son is not, but he is somewhat attached to mum, as Italians are wont to be, especially since Papa died, who was a really nice man. And so the son abandoned his studies and helps mum run the café.

And so I like going back there since I used to go there many years ago when I was still single. And she greets me warmly and asks me what I want, and it is nearly always the same thing, and that's melted cheese on toast with a poached egg.

DELICIOUS.

So I read the papers and that's dangerous to start since it's full of everything I detest. Nearly everything. And I wonder why everybody isn't as nauseated as me, and maybe they are, but just swallow the bilge as if it's something you have to endure, put up with, like dog-shit on the pavement. You don't have to step in it though.

What got up my nose was all the news about the Oscars. For thirty straight days I have had to see the same idiot tart since they were in the running for an Oscar, as if this was going to save our fetid ruin of a nation, and give us the pride we needed, a big, whopping boost up the jacksie for our ego. So now for thirty or more straight days I've had this woman's face shoved down my throat in every different position, with every different grin, grimace, sneer, chuckle, chortle, quip, every fucking day for the last thirty fucking days, if not more, England's fave dame, a lovely pudding who can do no wrong, since she is so unthreatening like a pudding. The Brits seem to fear beautiful sexy women and conspire to keep them on the margins as if they present something we feel we're not entitled to, something beautiful, exotic, lascivious, delicious ... but no, no, no give us puddings.

Oh how lovely they are and all they ever seem to play are stiff-necked, stiff-bodiced queens with lovely upper-class accents. And it's not the bitches' fault since they are stereotyped into that position. So this got up my nose somewhat, for today yet again, here was her face, her long dress, her asinine comments, and yet she is a nice old bird. But what I did on stage each night, on one night, was more demanding than the whole effing film. That film was made over a year ago and is still bowing and scraping. And what is film acting compared to stage acting? You cannot even begin to hold a candle to it. Not even a pathetic glimmer.

No!

With some exceptions if you like. Yes ... I'll give you just a few. But filming is like sprinting a hundred yards, then going in your trailer, having a coffee, a fag, having your bum wiped thoroughly with the director's tongue, resting.

Whereas on the stage you run a marathon, with maybe a break after 90 minutes, and then another hour of slogging. And naked, bare, exposed in front of live, critical, intelligent human beings. So on stage you do the marathon in a each night, and on film you do the marathon in 100 yard spurts, but you give the impression, at least film does, that you have done the entire marathon in one go. That's what film actors do. Each day as I go through sweat and fear followed by pleasure, relief and then anxiety again, more sweat and fear, the movie actor sits in a trailer and orders cappuccinos. With fucking chocolate.

So I've had enough of this actress or that actress or those actresses (especially the fat one with the perma-grin) and yet this is the way they are presented to us and how they feel they must present themselves and yet they may be perfectly nice people. Fuck 'em! For now they're making me sick, and not only me ... And there's the creepy-arsed director behind her who has made a good living directing mediocre shit and yet astonishingly keeps working. I can never figure that one out.

My food came and I managed to step out of the swampland of frustration of hate and enjoy my breakfast. Yes, that was nice. Oh yes that was nice and so I folded the paper and was amazed at how weird the British race was, allowing the government to corrupt the entire land with gambling casinos as if this was the best thing that could happen to us. Why doesn't it just sell cocaine outside schools? At least people will get some value out of that. I paid for my breakfast and walked home.

CHAPTER 4

An actor's life for me

On the days when you perform, the air and the hours have a completely different weight. You're aware of them and you refer to your watch far too often. The morning hours contain freedom and relaxation, a little frolic, and maybe if you can be bothered, a walk to the gym and some laborious swimming up and down, up and down. And yet swimming was one thing I used to love, in the outdoor pool in the summer before they closed it down, like they closed everything down that gave pleasure to the people. Like they closed all the cinemas down and the little recreation parks for the kids down, and so all those things that keep an idle mind occupied and even fulfilled are kept down. And how that local lido saved me as a child from a blighted horrible post-war London, from an indifferent father and a sweet but unhelpful mother, and it gave me a place and a purpose and pride and a joy and I would always go by myself and see mates there. I loved the swim and most of all the diving boards, and could do somersaults from the low springboard and would do them over and over again. Dive, tuck in, land feet first, climb out and take your turn, again, again, again ... and it was wonderful, and your appetite was wonderful.

DOWN! DOWN! DOWN!

It was so simple, too simple, but they had to close it down, and now you have to join an expensive gym and swim up and down with silent swimmers.

I even fantasised about being a competition swimmer but then my family moved to a different part of London, to a loathsome school in Hackney and that's where I learned to smoke and be a bum, although to be fair I still swam in Tottenham lido and had a good friend called Barry who was lithe and handsome and sensitive. But sadly I lost touch with him when I started taking up acting and then seemed to meet and make friends with an endless line of pooftahs. Not sure why this was but it seemed to come with a territory since they were more sensitive to me, and knowledgeable and informative about all sorts of strange things, and so I went through a weird 'poofy' period although no poof myself, despite loving girls to the point of madness. Once I discovered girls and wore a smart suit that was it. That. Was. It. Yes.

I had another friend called Andy, who had golden blonde hair and was devilishly handsome, with blue eyes, a straight nose, a blinding sense of humour and a gift for cockney scat that was remarkable, and he felt he was already a bit of a star and liked the West End too much, and it eventually corrupted him, but his bluff was amazing since he was as weak as a puppy but strutted like a mini-gangster. At the Lyceum dance hall, which was very exciting in the olden days, he would strut with the hard guys. He loved himself so much that he even had little time for women. He died from leukaemia in his early twenties, but I know it was his lifestyle that was rotten and had caused it. He couldn't bluff leukaemia.

I went home and made a cup of tea although I had just had two cups in the café, but it settled me as a coming home ritual, and fed my cat, who I adored and had kept for over ten years. It was a female tortoiseshell but it had only one good ear, the other having shrivelled up like a boxer's after an operation to reduce the swelling, but the cat didn't mind too much since it got a lot of attention, and as I sat in my basement room the cat would sit on the doorstep and wait for people to stop, pat her and say "What happened to your ear?"

So I ran a bath instead of going to the gym since I would feel good after a bath, and I still felt relaxed and contented after a night with my lover since she was young, scrumptious and lovely, and I usually fucked like my life depended on it. Yes, wonderful, but then I sped away in the morning. Early. In case she rings.

"How was the show?"

"Yeah, the show was good last night, really spot on, and the audiences are beginning to come in ... yeah, oh I was back late, so I missed your call ... went out with

Terry and Joe, yeah, for a Turkish, sure it was good, yeah, you ok? Yeah, ok call you later, bye darlin'... yeah, you too ... byyyyye."

The bath was relaxing and the time hadn't yet crawled towards the middle and so it was still 'freetime' — time without angst, without fear, and now after the bath and feeling calm I decided that a bit of exercise would be the right thing to do and a walk around the Islington streets would be in order, a brisk one, taking in Essex Road, up St Peter St, and then Upper St ... No didn't want to walk past that foul pub, scene of last night's 'triumphs'. So stick to a brisk walk to the market at Chapel St, get some shopping in, that would be both useful and worthwhile, and anyway I loved the market. Always have done. We all love markets but I really loved them and felt at home and never lonely there. When I was out of work, which was frequently, the only place I could go and not feel guilty were the gym and the market. Or having sex. Things that were fundamental, that didn't feel like I was time wasting, 'being' unemployed. That was the worst world to be in, the world of the unemployed, but that was the lot of actors, and so endure it and use the time. Don't feel such a sense of shame. How easily that button is pressed. Now I had decided to make my own work. Not to rely on the agent or some faggoty director, but to rent a room above a pub and gather a few likeminded mates and do a 'workshop'. That's what I was doing. Now as I was in fact working, albeit for only a couple of weeks more, I didn't feel so much the aching need, but I would get back to it for it was the best thing in the world to be in charge of

YOUR OWN FATE.

I strolled through the market and liked the rough old faces of the stall holders, some of whom greet me with familiar fondness since some time ago I had played some twaddle in some ghastly TV shit the like of which I could not believe. Such shit that I could barely learn the lines, such shit that invited only the shit to play the principals each week. Such shit that those same actors for no reason in the world turned against me. The shits. Such shit that they took no interest when I spoke of the workshop I was going to start and the wonderful plays they would work on. Such shit that even one of the girls went to the producer and accused me of 'pinching her bum' when I only touched it, brushed passed it accidently in a crowded lift. Such shit that I would be happy never to see that shit ever again. But that's why the stall holders waved. The work was pure, unadulterated puke etched all the way through like rotten Brighton rock. It stank to high heaven but it provided funds to do the workshop.

And there were REPEATS!

The poor little market was struggling along since there were so many upmarket foodie shops in N1 now, but it was still a pleasure to drift down and feast my eyes on the tumbles of fruit and veg and crap clothes and leather trash and greasy-spoon cafés and flower stalls, and it was still a vital part of Islington that had been there for eons and was never likely to vanish, at least not in this lifetime. And it was here that I used to take my girlfriends on Sunday morning, and sit in a little café run by a couple of Italian twins who sold ice cream and they were always pleased to see me and made us welcome. So we'd sit on stools by the window and read the Sunday papers, and I'd always order the same thing which was a sausage bap crammed with salad, and it always tasted heavenly. And when I looked out of the window I could always see the same man, ruddy faced and wearing glasses with milk-bottle lenses, selling cheap vegetables. He was always there, every day, winter and summer, and he never seemed to change. He had a mop of flaxen hair and had such a benign demeanour it was almost saintly. And I passed by his stall and smiled, and he always smiled back, and like everything, I compared my desultory work load with this market warrior who worked each and every day, in rain or sun, winter or summer. What was I, I thought, my part time wanking around compared to this Trojan, and sometimes I couldn't even look at him I felt so ashamed. But that would change. Yes. It would.

So I bought my veg and shopped around for other bits, like cheese and some mince to maybe make pasta and cat food and headed for home. At least it was my own home and that was something to be proud of these days. I bought it when, as a tenant, the house came on the market and it was dirt cheap because the house was full of sitting tenants, since in those days Islington was a slum with cheap housing for people who were on the dole. And so with a friend coming in for the deposit I was able to get a mortgage. I eventually paid my friend off and let one of the rooms, and lo and behold most of the mortgage was paid in this fashion. And I learned to live with others and wash my dishes after I had eaten and not leave a mess for the tenant and vice versa.

Mum came now and again and the cat liked her and would jump on her lap, but Dad never once visited since he had no interest in me or what I did. He always called me a bum, useless, and that he would rather die than take a penny from me when I once dared to insinuate that one day I'd be keeping him. His loathing for me knew no limits and yet, for the life of me, I could never make out why, nor could my sister or mother. None of us. I had a theory that I was never wanted and somehow interfered with his plans since it was no secret that he had a mistress on the side.

So I slowly walked back since I had lots of time and threaded my way through Camden Passage where the little shops and the small stallholders were out. I could waste a little more time thumbing through the bric-a-brac which was an unending source of fascination for me, for here was the residue of history, here the clues to the past, the shrouds of ghosts, old lenses, negatives on glass, beautiful pocket watches, art deco tea sets, art nouveau lamps, temptations and lascivious ornaments. Here I could bury time, get lost in time, until after a while with so many Wednesdays and Saturdays spent here people started to wave and smile as if I was a dealer myself, or part of the fabric of those few hundred yards, since I was always and invariably there ... invariably there ... watched it change and become missed.

And there I would take my lover Annie on whom and within whom was spurted much of a mutual interest, so to speak; and here was a market we could both roam because markets have what nowhere else has, and you plunge into the emblems and tokens of dead time and it can be quite moving. And climb up the stairs in the part of the market which dips down towards the back and on the second floor was another little café, but this one run by a gigantic woman with an outsize voice and manner to go with it, which was intimidating but she was good hearted and meant well and was what you might call a 'character'. There were just so many

CHARACTERS

round there within our small world, within the world where I floated like an asteroid, aimlessly floating.

And so I walked through that day, but the market had shrunken somewhat since the filthy profiteers who owned the buildings, seeing how the small entrepreneurs thrived, decided to increase the rents and forced the small people out to get the richer ones in, but that destroyed the character of the market since the richer ones tended to be run by faceless managers. I walked through it, recalled Annie and slid down the road to home.

CHAPTER 5

My home is my castle

———

It was a good Victorian house that I came on by chance when living with Alison in the same area, and it was while I was living with her that the agents with whom I had put down my name as a prospective tenant called and said that they had an unfurnished flat to let on two floors. And it was really perfect, but then I was living with Alison and it was a bit of struggle, since while I loved living with Alison I was dying to have my own home for the first time in my life.

I took it on and immediately advertised for a tenant to help pay the rent and look after the flat on my occasional stints in rep. I loved this house and slowly and gradually started putting it together and that was such great fun, such a wonderful sense of belonging to something, and that something belonging to you.

The first cup of tea, and yes, the stove works, and the lights also, and I even made a bed. I bought the wood from the wood-yard in Essex Road, made careful drawings of the dimensions, and although was useless at carpentry at school, suddenly found that indeed I could put pieces of wood together and sand them down, and so the bed was made, and then the shelves. The shelves were drawn first by an architect friend of Alison and he showed me how to make these beautiful interlocking shelves, and they were beautiful, and I was so, so, so proud of my workmanship. For the uprights were to the ceiling, the plywood shelves held them together, and at the end I was so, so, so very

PROUD!

One day Alison's other friend, an architect called Alistair, became my friend, and my new friend made me the most beautiful desk in the world. So beautiful you cannot imagine. It was long and fixed to the wall and the surface was scalloped at the end and really heavy and thick, almost swept back and dreamlike. At the end he had made two or three heavy drawers and one scooped out cupboard. It was strong, masculine and had such power and integrity. An architect's desk and I loved him for making me such a masterpiece. And that desk stayed with me and lived with me for years and it makes me feel proud, and menschlike to sit at such a great desk, and it even inspired me to write, which I do from time to time on my little portable typewriter since I loathe fucking laptops and computers and the look of them, and the people who sit and use them in cafés and bars and planes.

Now Alistair also made me a seating unit for the

kitchen which was in the shape of an L and was also boldly made with great wooden pine struts for the seat which would have cushions on them. And this kitchen unit was also magnificent and every piece of wood was beautifully shaped and the ends were sanded to a curve and you could get a lot of people round it which I did once, or maybe twice.

The first time I invited a lot of actors but I found myself running around a lot and not actually talking to the people I wanted to talk to, but it was nice for everyone else even if I not only wasn't involved, but needn't have even been there.

What really made the kitchen special was the installation of a black stove, and that was really magnificent since for years I had made do with a gas fire which needed feeding from the meter; but one day the meter jammed, for some reason I never knew and then for years I had FREE GAS. That was a gift and a godsend but the stove was really so very special and I could leave a pot of veg and meat on top of the stove, in the winter of course, and by the time I came back I had the most wonderful stew!

I loved my kitchen and had many memorable meals there and entertained many charming young women there as well. And at the back was the garden, slightly neglected since I was never a horticulture expert, and from the kitchen I could look out at the garden through the small window. But that was all to change. It was when I was impressing this sweet addiction called Helen that I decided to have the kitchen extended and the wall taken out and a large sliding door across the room, and that was truly magnificent, just wonderful, and so the slightly raised area became the kitchen area with a beautiful long bench dividing the room, and the stove and sink behind it, and that was something I once could only have dreamed of.

Oh now my house was becoming a wonderful dream house, and I had central heating whereas before I would have to walk down the road with my five gallon empty can and get it filled from the Welsh shop with that blue oil for my paraffin heater. Mind you those paraffin heaters were very romantic and gave off a lovely glow at night but you had to be careful and I had them for many years, many years of wearily schlepping a heavy can back to the house and then putting a funnel over the heater and filling it, and of course one must trim the wick. But my bedroom was still my bed/living room in the basement and that was cosy and instead of curtains I had wooden blinds like shutters attached to the walls, partly on account of some yobs throwing a brick through my window.

Alistair was a good pal and was skilled, creative, thoughtful, sensitive, and one day I introduced him to an Ex who worked in a bookshop in Camden Passage and they were both smitten and he pushed two or three kids out of the poor cow, but he eventually became hippyfied down in Devon where he built his own house and loved his beautiful, friendly black dog that I actually gave him one Xmas. Me and Alison spent a strange Xmas down there and went for a long cold walk after a well-meaning but soggy veggie lunch and he had his dog on a string leash like some poor sodden gypsy. I recall that the only pleasant thing was that the dog climbed on our bed and I could cuddle him, which did annoy Alison somewhat. But the walks were good by the refreshing, bracing roaring sea, but I was glad to get back on the effing train to London. So very glad.

My ground floor was the tour de force, my dream space, the king room of the house since it was a double room on the second floor from one end of the house to the other, with double doors in the centre which could close and then make two rooms.

Now Alistair didn't make anything for that large room so I mostly cobbled it together myself. I put a large wooden table against the wall in the back room which became my second desk, since I now needed a spare room once the tarts started living with me. And against the wall I had a notice board made of cork upon which I would attach various bits of info which tended to stay there long after the reason for their existence had expired. A low single bed which kind of doubled for a sofa, and which I made, was situated behind me and I quite liked sleeping there sometimes since I had a view of the garden.

In the front room I had a couple of armchairs, coffee table, and at the far end a great leather sofa which I once bought in Camden passage and had for years. And of course a telly without which I don't think I could exist. Also in the recess I had tried to build shelves after a fashion and here I had my record player and tuner and tape deck. A large poster of a native Indian was carelessly pinned to the wall and I had blinds this time on the front window with a giant flying balloon such as was popular in France at the end of the last century.

This is all I needed. It was my shag pad and sanctuary, workshop, home, den, zoo, for at one time I had three cats and all were quite beautiful, and all got on well together since I wouldn't tolerate any aggression between them.

So that's just a brief intro to the house, but the house was much more than that, so very much more. An escape sometimes, a hideaway, my pride and joy, my house,

MINE!

And I could do what I liked with it. One day I was doing a show and there was a young vibrant woman in it, an American as a matter of fact, of European descent with large deeply brown eyes and long luxuriant hair and she came over one day and we took it from there. And one day she called and invited me to have lunch which she offered to cook, and so she came round and we cooked rather tasty Chinese chicken in a wok and had lots of fun. And so, one day she needed a room to rent, and so she did, on the second floor, and of course popped down for a cuddle from time to time, but I was never what you might say excited by her at the beginning, but it grew, and then eventually I was, and so she moved into my part of the house and before I could say crabs and lice she and I were spliced!

Now this was an event for me to be married to a woman I still desired and so this felt like it was getting real for once. Except we got married for economic and political reasons since she claimed her work permit had expired and she would have to marry Someone or Anyone to protect her status, and so I thought well we had been living together for a couple of years so what the hell, and so we did. And she was a really sweet and charming girl, but she couldn't really cook so we ate out a lot, and it didn't seem to matter since she was so accomplished at so many other things.

Now having few friends, or real and deep loving friends, or reliable friends since Alistair was now a hippy in Devon, I was at a loss for a best man at the registry office, but as luck would have it I was doing a play at a small theatre in South London, and so I went round the cast one night, asking if they were free in the morning, since I was getting married and one-by-one they had unfortunately other engagements. One was doing an important yoga class, another was seeing his doctor, but one, who was also quite a good friend, said he would be very happy to be best man, and one of the women also agreed, so we had two, and it was really nice of them to come and a further bonus was that it was the last night of the show and so we had a last night party, and so this doubled as a wedding feast ... haha!

And when I told folks that we just got married they all laughed and thought I was joking since it was all so modest, but what the hell did it matter. It didn't have to be like some gross untalented slagheap who marries for money and sells her wedding to Hello magazine for a million. That marriage is doomed to death. Ours was lovely and she was so happy she burst into tears at the registry office. Actually what brought on the tears was hearing my middle name read out, which was a bit of a soppy one. Then we went to Mum's and told her and she was well chuffed and made us lunch, and we fell asleep on the sofa.

But that was then, and it lasted less than six years, but they were long nourishing years and bore much fruit, if not baby fruit since she did get pregnant one day, but didn't wish to have a baby just yet for a number of reasons not least that it might totally hamper her career as a dancer, which considering just how much she had worked on it, wasn't as superficial as it might seem. But alas she did it and I remember seeing her back disappearing round the corner and wishing into myself the courage to say "Don't do it"… but I had caused so many damn abortions I had lost count, and why didn't they take bloody precautions, for they must know that men are totally without any sense of responsibility or intelligence. Once the cock hardens it seems to freeze the brain. Guaranteed brain freeze.

And now she's gone, long gone.

CHAPTER 6

Killing nothing but time

The day passed and I prepared something for later after the show which seemed to calm me somewhat as if the preparation was the secret to tranquilising the nerves. Then I cleared up my rooms, read a bit more of a book that was obsessing me, 'The Conquest of Mexico' by Bernal Diaz, then had a nice long hot bath. Is this the second one? Looked at the time. Looked at the time. The time.

TIME.

It was nearly time.

Yes, time to take a slow walk down the road ... slowly, take your time. I hate this time, I hate this time of the day when you're just going in, when you're travelling to the place of execution, the torture chamber. And this is that time, the hour or so before, then the hour before, and then the half hour before, and then you slowly start revving up, slowly for this time you are exchanging various chemicals in your body, slowly but surely endorphins are sizzling and adrenalin is getting warmed up, and the guts are tightening, and the concentration is narrowing and focusing and the lines are now being run and lighting up the neuro-transmitter, and the courage is only very slightly seeping into your stomach, and the heart is just beating only a tad more speedily and I am again at the church opposite the small seedy stinking pub and watching the few punters going in and ten minutes before the 'off' I will walk across and swiftly slide through the soggy flesh of the punters, slide through since

I HAVE A MISSION!

A soldier of the theatre, you are primed, getting ready, steamed up, alert as a vampire, oh, you are dangerous and so you cross the road and look at the crumbly old building so neglected. But it can still kick arse in that back room unlike the soggy yuppie shithole round the corner with its hanging terracotta flower pots and shitty, dead-hearted shows and its long lists of patrons and investors that it woos with such passion, and yet the place is a symbol of death.

Or maybe it's because they never ask for me, so maybe my acidic feelings are intensified, but they did discuss it once. Yes, something quite major, and then reneged on the deal. Yuppie trash always do that. Always.

I'm in the little back stage area and all the actors are there and greet, and I swiftly change and step into the yard for a quick roll-up. And the stage manager calls the five and we're all revving and then he calls beginners and you may be sure that all our heads are little line machines just going over a scene or two to confidence us for the night.

"We've got clearance".

We walk on and get to our places. The fear has gone replaced by a cold deadly challenge. The music kicks in with the lights and then two whole minutes of frenzy! The roles were based on real people. Real actors in fact who were in a movie, and one of the actors, a disgruntled player, wrote a play about his fellow actors which was in a way quite a cool thing to do and so the film gave birth to a little writhing bastard of a play which was indeed much better than the film since it sliced into their viscera and revealed the organs whereas the film only revealed the muscles of the protagonist.

So in the play there was a perpetual but energetic loser who was splendidly played by a lovely actor and then there was the dreary pragmatist played by a good Scots actor who tended toward sullen. Then a brute of a beast who took the part of the 'heavy' who was always and only talking about 'pussy' and describing his pussy delights and this was played by a huge heavyweight who was darned good and there was me. I was cast as the outsider, the actor who couldn't get on with anyone, made friends with no one and watched, always watching and thinking, observing and describing his lunch very eloquently. And then there was the actress who played the 'bird'. Oh yes. There was her and she was so beautiful, so very lovely, and sexy and fresh, and gorgeous, and I really liked her a lot ...

BUT, BUT, BUT...

I was married and living with a bitch and that was good, yes, very good ... in a way ... but hell it certainly tied you up, didn't it, and so I could only flirt with her ... just flirt, and I knew that she liked me ... really knew that she had a thing for me, but I had to let it go since it made playing that much easier, and what do you know ... in the end the nice actor whom I got on with so well scored with the girl and they ended up living together. So in a way that was a loss, but we got on better like that ... I guess. I think by living together unless you are really in love and still pumping some nights, you can lose a lot of adventure. Yeah...

The show went well tonight, went really well, and at the end there was a lot of cheers, a lot, and yes, some critical bitches had slated it, misled their readers, lied, twisted the story, soured the plot, and yet the play was so simple, about loneliness, just a desire for a little company. The writer was a nice enough guy and could be funny one day and utterly remote the next but I got on with him alright since he could talk to me about his 'bugs.'

And we all gathered on the pavement after since it was

a lovely warm summer, and we sniffed the warm air and inhaled the roasted garlic wafting down the road from the Greek cafés. And I had friends, since the actors were my friends apart from the sullen one who always shot off. So we stood there and chatted, revved up with the joy of having completed the show, and enlivened and happy, and in that good mood I made it home.

The light was on since my wife had come back early from the nursing and was happy to see me and had made a salad from what I'd bought, guessing that I would be coming home that night. And I told her about the show and how it went and who was in and the laughs I got, and how the actors were coping, and who was a bit moody, and then she told me her story. After, we watched a bit of telly and went to bed. Then in bed she tells me how she's fed up with the nursing gig and wants to sing since she has a really bravura voice and sings jazz and so I said hey, give it a go. And turned over and went to sleep...

CHAPTER 7

Risk, relief, repeat

I went to sleep and dreamed. Often of my mother, especially when I am a little disturbed, but I hate and loathe dreaming of my mother because there's always shit in the bed – in the dream of course – and that frankly is horrible. Just too horrible, smears of shit on the sheets ... why do I dream such horrid things ... maybe because my wife is turning into my mother ... oh, oh, oh!?! Not good, but not altogether terrible. I'm a pragmatist. But that dream comes only in batches and then my dreams are clean and pure and loving and often I dream of lovely girls whom I am amorously kissing, and I adore these dreams because frankly I hate married life with a vengeance.

It's ok for a while and so loving when you need each other and I am working on a show and she's there to take care of the house and me, and waiting up with a wonderful meal, and we are all cosy and watch the TV and put on weight. But then I meet someone so beautiful who desires me, and me them, and I have to bury all these feelings, or do it circumspectly and that creates a problem since you are limited in the times you are free and when she wants you and needs you. And you need her just as much, and you can't really, you just can't hurt the woman you live with

BECAUSE YOU HAVE DONE IT TOO MANY TIMES BEFORE.

Too many times before and it hurt, yes it hurt so much and caused so much pain but if you remember, it was always good after you did the deed. Then it was good and you felt so free and happy and the pain just disappeared. When you took the risk! And you were free, and what a relief, what a sweet relief.

But how have you got yourself bound up again like with a mummy? Ugh. It's always the same and the sensation and desire all but disappears so why go through it again and lose yet another home. So you may as well stay as you are since you do care for each other and have something on the side, but that doesn't always work since the one on the side begins to get attached, since that's what sex does to you. It's such an abandonment of the senses, such a naked freeing of the soul, so raw and open, and the greatest sensation on earth and heightened all the more when it is rare, rationed, has to be sneaked in a furtive afternoon, how lusciously lascivious.

When it is rare, and oh how you suffer when you

can't make the time, when you can't just get out of the fucking house cause the bitch is there and always there, always and ever there, there, there … Except for the rare occasion she's called out of town. And you can't just say, "Hey I'm going to see Bobby", cause you don't know a Bobby, but you do know some, but you feel guilty and the guilt streams off your face like the surface of a cup of tea when it curdled and made a skin like it did in the old days before they tampered with the milk, and so how many women have you had to pass on, oh how many lovely women … so many lovely women!!!

There was Katherine, there was Saskia, there was Deborah, and on and on, but once, just once, I did get so involved that I fell from my tree and this is what I never ever wanted to do since I was in control of my fate, and this is what I definitely did not want to do, but I did it, and it came to pass that my wife clearly saw that I was disturbed and I had to confess that I'd tumbled from my tree and not for the first time either.

I fell off the tree because I was holding on by a few thin branches, seeing her when my wife was away which was so rarely so it became

SPECIAL

just to see her, but something also inside me never wanted to leave my wife, because I liked being with her the best of all, had more depth of feeling and the day to day reality, earnestness, comfort, friendship and mental stimulation.

To be frank the woman I fell in love with had the brains of a goldfish and that's giving her credit. She was so sweet and loving and delicious and pretty and sexy but as empty as an empty jam jar. Never had I seen or heard anything so empty, vacant, sterile and worst of all, far worse, were her empty friends. The vacuous, tarty models that she caromed around with and sometimes I felt such a sense of self disgust when I thought of my poor wife alone at home while I was with those festering vacant maggots. I know, poor me. But because I couldn't see my tart as much as I would like, I developed a bit of an obsession for her. Now this grew into a grand passion when she naturally threatened to leave since she wouldn't be a second-hand tart that I only saw when I was available. Naturally she wanted more, very much more, and she threatened to leave and then whack! It hit me like a club to my nuts. I fell off the tree.

And now my missus knew but seeing I was so distressed she actually felt more compassion than anger, for that was the kind woman she is and was. She became concerned for my mental health and watched over me like a hawk, and she said:

"Since you only see her on odd occasions it doesn't give you time to see what a manipulative cow she might be, and probably is, so why not spend time with her at Xmas instead of you and I spending it together. I'll go home to my family in France and you can spend Xmas and New Year and see how you get on…"

That seemed fair enough and my lover was pleased

that I would spend Xmas with her folks in the country and she was preparing a big Xmas eve party and food in her flat and so I went, picking up a couple of bottles of champagne on the way.

When I got there, there was a sour atmosphere in the air, but that was just the smell of her rancid friends whose brain cells were stagnating so I tried to get through the evening, tried to chatter to the monsters, tried to be pleasant, ate some of the rotten food. Then something odd happened. There was a guy there who was somehow wishing to provoke me, an actor who once had a smidge of success a few years back and had done fuck-all since, but he must have at some time fucked my lover since they were kinda sweet together and he had brought round some party things.

Well as chance would have it, I was on the telly that night in quite a good role in a very touching little play. So we all piled into the bedroom where she had the only telly and watched, but this arrogant cock couldn't stop making idiot insidious remarks about my performance which I chose to ignore believing that he was probably stoned. At the end of the evening he could not but help making another tacky jokey comment which then had me react in no uncertain manner, he had no right to be making any fucking remarks, and delivered with the best venom I could muster. Which then caused him to turn on his heel and get out.

The evening then got progressively viler as the plan was now to go to a local disco and though I loved dancing,

I didn't dance, I couldn't dance, but just hung around. Just hung around, hung around and watched, like a visitor to the monkey cage. And then we went back to her dull flat and went to bed, I couldn't touch her but somehow managed to get to sleep.

In the morning I got up early and went downstairs and there was the largest mound of caked-up plates and glasses and pots and pans that I had ever seen, but I got to work and washed the fucking lot, but when she came downstairs she didn't appear to notice but just made coffee and I mumbled something appreciative since I was trying to make up for the lousy evening which I had thoroughly spoilt.

And then we went to her folk's home in the country which had to be one of the dreariest Xmas's I have ever spent in my entire life. As horrible as it was possible to be, since there was not of lot of affection going around, although her mother was a nice elegant lady.

Then I drove my nice old second-hand Jag home to her flat and stayed in the car and drove myself home, and was *so happy to be home alone. So happy. Alone.*

CLEAR THINKING.

CHAPTER 8

The impotent performer

Ah, but then the new year was zooming up and I wanted to spend the following days in the countryside with her so we could go for walks and really spend time together since she had always said that this is the thing she wanted most of all and that I was not giving her. So now let's do it but, now she says she has plans to go to Paris!! So fuck her, and maybe she was right and had had enough, so let her be vacuous and frivolous with her seedy trash mates and leave me alone. And alone I was; alone, and very much alone. *But did it teach me a lesson?*

NO.

I continued to chase and woo and court her unto sickness.

But then a new and bewildering phenomena took place ... I found that I could no longer fuck her! I found that I was becoming intimidated by her, afraid I couldn't please her, I couldn't whip up into a storm of desire, I couldn't keep my member hard and stiff for her. I felt insecure with her since she made me feel so insecure, and she started to grow more beautiful in my eyes, and more desirable, and I wanted so much to please her and I was becoming weaker and weaker in my desire to please, in my intimidated position.

I had not felt anything like this for the two years we had been raunching around. I was always able to fuck her even if it was a little like fucking a corpse because she hardly moved and had no life in her cunt. It was like a vast empty hole but I still was able to fuck and enjoy her, but there was definitely something missing. Usually women have active, pulsing little pussies and can do all sorts of things with them. They are live little creatures down there. But she just had a still dead thing. And then she started to object to french kissing which is so sweet with a woman and so loving. But I was still becoming fixated since I felt she might leave me, or fuck others.

Then she went to L.A. where all the movie phonies hang out and then I had the 4pm trauma since I couldn't phone before then, being 8am there, and then we had all sorts of bizarre calls and I was growing more and more and more insane.

Then I actually went out there and it was horrible, monstrously horrible, and I should have known it much, much earlier. I believed that if she was gentle and sweet and understood that this was just a phase then our sex and passion would return, but she had no time for that and just couldn't *help. She could not help.* NOTHING. Just that empty, idiotic upper class voice saying "It's ok. I'd prefer a cuddle", and then turn over and sleep and I lay there in a swamp of regret and failure.

I was always hard with her and as soon as I tried to penetrate the bone went straight out of it! As if maybe my subconscious knew that there was something evil in her and it didn't want to go there. Maybe it *knew* and I didn't. They say men think with their cocks. I should have listened.

Eventually I broke down and cried in front of her and just got out of the bed and went to my hotel and I started very slowly to get better and at the end I had my darling wife to return to, and I felt clean and strong and pure again. Once I got that viper and her poison out of my system.

CHAPTER 9

The yeast always rises

Oh how it made me ill, for so many months, just ill because there is something about losing yourself to a woman until she holds the strings of your guts and pulls this way and that and it's not good but it comes from some terrible deep-seated insecurity. Something that happened in childhood, some terrible sense of loss and when it comes up (no pun intended), when there's maybe a threat suddenly, all those tapes are replayed with a vengeance.

MADNESS.

I was impotent for the best part of a year after that incident until I got to trust women again, and when I did, and when I found a young woman and it didn't work the first time round, I didn't freak out or duck the issue, but simply said to her, please, please be patient ... just wait a little and be patient, and she was. She was loving and patient and tender, and lo and behold my yeast started to rise again and my spunk flew out of me and life flew back in. Not quite as it did but I was getting better because now I had a real soft and loving woman, and then it worked, it worked, and I was coming to life again ... Thank god. Yes thank god! Perhaps he is a man.

Now I'm free, that was a bad one although in the early days she did have sweet and loving qualities and when I was away working I wrote loving letters to her and she wrote back and we were both in love, but then I became 'weak' and she said to a mutual friend that she liked me when I was 'strong' and not so *needy*. Ah well, I will learn not to be so needy ever again but much as I tried it did happen once again.

But now I am calm. I have never been so calm.

This was a beast, a phantom and I am glad. So glad that it ended. I woke early and got up quietly and made some tea and looked at the bright blue misty summer morning and it was good. There was one small puffy cloud and the sun was just nibbling at the edge of it.

I stroked the cats and they arched their backs and lifted their tails and were so appreciative of a bit of cuddling and then I opened a tin of cat food and they pounced on it with great enthusiasm and then I walked upstairs and got the paper and took it back down to the basement and then decided to have a pee and it came out in a strong, manly whoosh, so then I washed my hands and face and brushed my teeth.

My teeth looked clean and strong and they were

always my pride, my teeth, and my strong white teeth. Women like men with strong white teeth, not stained, not crumbled, not brown, or with black bits, because the teeth seem to symbolise the man. Clean strong, healthy and white. Didn't always have good teeth since poor Mum knowing little about these things fed me a lot of cakes and sweet things and maybe I wasn't so devoted to keeping my teeth healthy and so was always going to the dentist from a young age, and getting great metal fillings. But now I take far more care.

I turned on the radio and some soothing classical music oozed out, with lots of brass and some thin high choir music. I sat and opened the paper. Some rich untalented tart, who may be a really nice person, is getting married twice. Once in England and once in India, since her poor pussy-whipped boyfriend is rich and Indian. I feel sorry for him already, and she's got him to make an entrance on a white horse. Maybe like Emiliano Zapata!

Her being has acted like a poultice drawing the scum of London to her 'do', a whole array of talent. I'm sure they may be very nice people but I cannot swallow the excrement that is put out now, the way the arse-licking British press constantly expose their unfortunate grimaces since it's not their fault we're living in the eye of the mediocre storm that's galvanising the nation. *Shit's in big time*!

And so these nice people are all together at this wedding of this woman. There was a picture of a woman there whom I knew and who nearly drove me insane, she's so insane herself. Insanity breeds insanity.

Then again, on the next page there was a journalist bitch that for some mysterious reason likened grey squirrels to rats! And mocks a group of well-meaning animal lovers for saving some who had been born prematurely. She says they should be killed ... the squirrels ... and for what reason ... cause they eat bulbs! It's amazing how many bitches writing for the press seem to wish to show their tough unsentimental side. Not soppy tarts us! Nah, we can kill and hunt with the best of men. And during the anti-hunting debate, how many said that while not supporting hunting, that they didn't much care for the little verminous creatures. And all this from women whom I used to believe were higher up the spiritual ladder than men. *How wrong I was. Yes, how wrong!!*

And that other tart who was appalled that people objected to the use of animals for experiments to try and find some cure for some evil disease, since apes and monkeys are of a lower order than humans, and how vile these animal campaigners are. Well, I detest the idea of my life being extended in any way by the wholesale slaughter of animals. Rather live five years less than the abuse of one single monkey with a prod stuck in its brain. Not for me Miss, so go fuck yourself!

But what I can't get for the life of me is why more people aren't feeling, thinking the same thing when it's so bloody obvious how horrible it is. When I think of poor rabbits being tortured with lotions smeared over their eyes I wonder why there isn't a fucking revolution to

>STOP THIS FUCKING TORTURE!
>STOP TORTURING ANIMALS!

CHAPTER 10

Expressing ourselves

She's up. Up and about. She's taken a croissant out of the freezer and turned the oven on. Then she grinds some coffee since she loves that first thing in the morning, the kettle is filled and swiftly boils and the coffee is poured into the cafetiere, then she pushes the plunger down. She pours the coffee and then dribbles in some milk and a spoonful of honey, checks the croissant ... not done yet ... then she asks for a bit of the paper and these are the first words she's uttered ... I pass over the magazine section and she starts reading.

She: You were snoring so loudly last night.
He: Me! My god have you heard yourself... it's frightening.
She: I didn't snore last night...
He: You did! I woke you, do you remember I woke you ...
She: You woke me?

He: Yeah, it was so loud I had to wake you ... you even woke the cat...

She: Well, your snoring was unbelievable. Thought you were going to die... you were breathing so funny, with your mouth open...

He: Your snoring is so loud, I'm amazed you don't wake up... it's cause you smoke too much... let alone the drinking...

She: You drink more than me...

He: Oh really, I'd be dead if I drank as much as you...

This is a form of married life.

This is the sweetest of conjugal bliss.

This is the torment of familiarity.

This is the hell you suffer so as not to return to an empty room and sit alone and prepare your supper.

I rang my friend Bruce who I met when I was working at the Citizens Theatre Glasgow. I liked Glasgow then before they tore down those wonderful buildings in the Gorbals. Now it's a veritable shithole and so I'm glad I had the opportunity to see its rawness and earthiness. I did three plays and I was terrific in two of them and one I couldn't get to grips with. One was a famous woman writer and the whole cast were so enamoured of her and couldn't wait to crawl up her arse that they had coffee with her before the show. Then on stage they all shit themselves knowing she was there and what she was like. Wisely I chose NOT to meet her until after the show and we got on fine and she said my performance was the best she had seen in the role, even better than the guy who did it in London!

Bruce was a nice warm hearted Aussie and we talked about starting our own little workshop where we could try out plays. This was quite a radical idea since actors were conditioned to be passive and wait for the phone to ring or have the occasional lunch with their agent. We wanted to change all that ... all that desperate waiting around and trying to fill your day ... and having our own workshop was the best way we knew of spending our valuable lives. Also it would train actors, keep their technique on alert, and they'd learn not to be so subservient to directors, most of whom are fucking useless anyway. And some are just downright criminal and those are the ones who seem to be the most successful!

So we found a pub round the corner with a large room upstairs which we would rent for two or three hours and Bruce had a few guys and girls lined up and it was to be Saturday from 2pm till 5pm. I was very excited, as excited as I have ever been in my life, as if my body sensed that this was the right path, scary and intimidating, but somehow the right thing to do. To express ourselves.

So now I had a goal, a reason to live beyond the finishing time of the play which everyone seemed to enjoy for there were cheers from the small house each night, even if the bitches didn't get it. It was a man's play, about men and their concerns and fears and also their aspirations and dreams. It was both gross and lyrical, sad and exhilarating, but bitches don't relate to each other the way men do and that's perfectly natural. Why should they? What is unacceptable is the way they constantly trumpet how much more open and giving they are to each other. How men are so tight and unable to reveal their emotions. Wrong! Wrong!

WRONG!

Men are careful about blubbing their emotions, about suffocating you, and choose carefully with whom they can be open, and if they can't they will chew on it and solve it themselves. Or write a play about it. Or compose a song, or get drunk, but they will not sit in a coffee shop swallowing gallons of skinny cappuccino and endlessly whining about their husbands.

Never mind and fuck it. The last night of the play came and everybody of course wondered about a last night celebration but nobody could make up their minds. In the end we decided to go to the Cuban café up the road and I just loved a caipirinha, that Brazilian fire water with crushed limes, sugar and ice. The night was good and everybody had a great time and the food was excellent and I was so happy since there is nothing in the world I like more than to sit in a café with my actor mates. That's really good. Yeah!

So now I was once more out of work... going for the odd audition when my agent could get me one, and how I tried. How I dreamed of one day doing Shakespeare at the RSC, treading the boards with the great actors, how I dreamed of it, like an unattainable fantasy. I did audition for one part and actually got a call back. I worked all week for four or five hours a day just on my two audition pieces but I had overworked it and didn't quite have the swing to the pieces. The response was cold, dismissive, dead, just like this director's work. But he had so many to see, and we actors are so self-centred and paranoid.

CHAPTER 11

The yapping hyena

Yes I've come to the conclusion that women are insane, which is not to say that they aren't delightful, talented, sensitive, loving, and delicious — but the craziness slowly creeps into them. Now, having been married quite a few years, it is not uncommon to have a flirtation or two and this of course goes both ways. However, there are some bitches out there who gradually demand more of you than you can give since I still love my wife and she is my ally, friend, mentor, companion, nurse, mother, sister and child all rolled into some curiously strange ball of needs and loves. But, the lover is a sexual being which is wonderful, delightful, sweet, charming, and so healthy. Temporarily at least. You give to your mistress treats, dinners, occasional trips, outings, money, advice, but beyond that you really cannot go. You cannot do more. Or give more. You cannot take her out on the weekends, or share Christmases, or introduce her to your few friends (since obviously they know my missus), and of course at the same time you would be spitting on your missus and that would be not only cruel, but deceitful. But the bitch wants this and she's getting greedy for more and sends abusive texts if I can't comply, with vile accusing attacks, and so it doesn't matter to her if she hurts another woman and while she rants and raves about her rights she is most willing to spit on others' rights. Yet she was the only sex I had for some time, and sex with her was so easy and the reason it was so easy and so delicious and so erotic and so sweet was simply because she was a mistress, because it was rare and special and limited it was

FANTASTIC!

And I could send horny dirty messages which turned her on and she loved them and I went to her filthy little flat which looked like it hadn't been cleaned in years, but it was comforting sex at first, since I had just come out of the previous terrible love affair. Then they go sour, and each for the same reason. And that is because I cannot and will not leave my wife.

Then they threaten and withdraw, and then I find that this triggers something like an emotive earthquake inside me and I promise the world and marriage and children, but when it comes to the crunch, drugged as I am with obsessive love, there is still a tiny worm of sense that gnaws away and prevents me from taking the last step.

I don't wish to go that way again. So this present bitch helped me, to turn me away from yearning after the other bitch, and so it went well at first and the sex became even better and silkier and lustier and all was well.

Then women like to claim territory, but a bit at a time, acting quite innocent at first and then slowly moving in, making claims, threatening sexual withdrawal unless certain demands are met, and so you give in to these demands, slowly, gradually, feeling of course always and forever guilty, since you are not able to give her your full attention. And so this guilt is twisted like a tourniquet round your throat.

Yet being a mistress can suit many women since the guy is not always breathing down their necks and you don't have to hear him snoring and smell his breath in the morning or pick up his stinking underwear.

So lovers only give the best of themselves usually. But this bitch is a mad one and once you give in, once they detect a spot of weakness, they go for it like starving hyenas. They really do go for the throat, leaving messages on your land line for the wife to hear. Muck about with your life and habits. And much as I miss the bitch's sex, and I do miss it like a limb has been taken from me, I will not tolerate it! Rather than give in yet again, which is unlikely since she is too weird a bitch to fall in love with – thank god for I do have a little tendency for that...

CHAPTER 12

I will outperform you all

I was hoping for a bit of TV work to tide things over but my agent was hopeless at getting me any and we have these constant chats about how much she believes in me and knows that things will change, but still little work. And on the rare occasion that you do get picked for some slovenly written role you can barely get your mouth round the junk, like it won't go down, it's so difficult to learn and you keep vomiting it up again with a reflex gagging action.

But at least you're active and going somewhere and meeting lots of people and exchanging crap pleasantries and going on location and meeting actors in the lobby of the hotel. And they're always drinking and then sniffing out who's on their wavelength and gradually you find yourself alone or with some old codger.

Sometimes though, some nice makeup girl will accompany you for a drink, and that leads to something pleasurable at the end of the day. Well, now there's nothing, and so we will make our own work. At last, and please god.

Saturday came round, the day we had planned for the workshop, and I was mighty excited just to get going again. I left the flat in high spirits and decided to have an early breakfast at the corner greasy-spoon Italian café which had faithfully served the neighbourhood for twenty years, year in, year out, cooking up the same old pleasant working class tasty crap along with some saucy Italian dishes. I could almost measure my life by this café. The first time I put a little show together I actually went and got the teas and coffees. Then my first real serious girlfriend was taken there, and then the second and the nice Italian lady got to know them all. And still I would go in there, winter or summer, and in summer she would put out one little table for me in that grotty little street, for me to enjoy breakfast 'al fresco'.

Then to the pub, and I saw my old mate Bruce and we went upstairs where chairs were set out and gradually everybody who had been invited turned up full of expectancy and enthusiasm coupled with an excitement that this would be, or at least might be, a life changing moment. So we all dutifully sat and Bruce made a tiny speech to the effect that this would be just a place to work out, try 'auditions' so that you would grow more confident having performed them in front of your peers. I thought this somewhat limited the scope I had in mind which was to find some play that we could work on together and perform it somewhere, and what play. But few if any of us had a clue. And so we just sat there and chatted a bit about what might be a worthwhile thing to pursue, and then one or two fags were lit and no one was doing anything but gabble about how they would search for a 'movement' person to give some classes and a 'voice' person, and whom we knew and blah, blah, fucking blah.

So I piped up and asked who might like to show us 'something', some piece they had in their 'repertoire' so to speak, and then we could comment and give positive notes, and all of us should go in turn. This led to several saying that they hadn't got anything prepared since they weren't expecting to be 'doing' anything like that and scratched their heads, while others said that they could, but it had been some time since they had 'auditioned' so they might be a bit scratchy ... And at this time I thought that this was the usual way of getting things going and that actors have to be encouraged and instructed, and even cajoled. But I also thought that they were behaving like tossers and were dying to get a workshop going in theory, but when it came to the crunch were too shit-scared to do anything.

So one or two got up and did some limpish pieces but at least they did get up and have a go. And that's when you strip yourself down, make yourself naked. Like I never understood why some actors have this passion for flashing their tackle when the very act of getting up in front of people is already baring yourself, your soul, your faults, your mind – to take your clothes off on top of that seems just a little teensy bit wanky.

Then I stood up and did one of my favourite pieces, a piece I adore from a play I would give my soul to do, but alas, it was not to be. A play that no idiot in the wanked-out, toe-rag, lick-spittled, yuppie-ridden Brit theatre could ever stage, or would ever stage. But one day I will, so help me god. Yes I will. But I shan't say just yet what the play is since it might put the mockers on me doing it. And the group seemed to really like it and we had a bit of a chat after. Then it was time to wind up.

So we all got up and said it was a productive first day and we'll all meet next week at the same time, and I was happy that we had actually gone this far and broken the ice, and made the first steps in forming our own company. Then Bruce and I had tea and chatted happily about our first cautious attempts to liberate ourselves.

Soon as I get home I am liable to get bored as a dead rat. I know too well what to expect, which used to be so nice and warm and cosy after work to come home to a nice drink made so lovingly with care, but now, now I was getting edgy ... need some pash.

PASH.

But with pash comes the sickness ... oh the terrible yearning and longing and needing and pining ... aaaaaah!

CHAPTER 13

The days pass

The days passed like they always passed when you don't have the night to do your work. The nights were good after the show and you felt like you had expanded yourself and reached parts of your being that were dormant and locked away, but then what with the nerves, the adrenalin charging, sluicing through your body, you come to life. Each night was like an epiphany and you glowed, you were spiritual, transcendental. It was wonderful and there is nothing in the world like it. Even if you suffered and sweated and felt like shit during the show, and you couldn't wait for the end, when the end did come then you were a completely different being. It's something like a glow within you, a divine purity, and you changed. Yes you did. You became what you should be, or could be. Alive in all senses of the word and that could last for hours and you clung to the feeling and wanted to celebrate that feeling with a feast, a drink with a friend, and then nothing was better. You were without guile or fear or anger, just floating in the bliss.

What could you do when you did not have the means to do this, when you were unemployed and just filling the day and chewing the hours and felt somewhat dead, numb, fearful, ordinary, and lifeless? What could you do to try and ignite that feeling again? What indeed could you do? The workshop was good, it was a beginning, a start, but then I have to wait a whole fucking week for the next one and become stale and dribble through the days trying not to nag my agent too much. Sex was good and was a means of igniting some of that feeling that left you purged and cleansed and inspired, but with the bitch at home it was difficult. Too difficult.

We ate and watched TV and had a few drinks and went to bed and in the morning she went to work to her part-time nursing job, and I went out to the breakfast café. I looked forward to the morning so I could get up and enjoy the taste of the new day and this morning I would go to the gym.

It's a chore to get there to the YMCA in Tottenham Court Road. Once I was there and in the gym I felt better and hoped I could get a game of handball which I loved and which would have the sweat pouring off me in no time. But the taxi drivers always had the same idea and took over the two courts and I had to wait and hope one of them would play me when they finished, and sometimes they did and then I had a good game. It's a good game handball and it's fast but these taxi drivers were unbelievable and played every day for years and you could barely score a point.

One had thick glasses and a real old English face and he allowed me to play against him while he was waiting for his partner and I just couldn't work out how he could get so good and so fast. Yet he was gentle and never boasted as he roasted you on the court. The others in the 'second division' I could beat, and beat easily, but there is that next step, the next step that you have to attain to be the best, to give them a run for their money, and I could not reach that step no matter how hard I tried. Then I would do some light weights, bench press and all that and have a welcome shower.

I would leave the gym feeling on top of the world and fit to do anything, run a marathon, climb a mountain, and most of all rehearse a play. Oh, how I was simply dying to rehearse a play, was bursting to rehearse a play, and to give not only my all but everything, my soul, my guts, blood and sweat. I went to auditions and did my all but was it too much, or not enough, or not 'English' enough, since I still had that trace of working class in me, just the merest trace.

I recall auditioning for some idiot from some large company that specialised in the classics, and how I worked until the day. I did the audition and actually got a call back which delighted me but was then eliminated! And by such a lazy director whose shows I saw and they were low, sloppy, disgusting and shoddy.

So I left the gym feeling light, drained of all impurities,

and as I left I saw the casting director in the street since they used the YMCA for rehearsal sometimes, and so I ran up to her. I said I would love a chance to audition again since my last was a year ago and she smiled weakly and said she would see if it were possible. Ah! What the hell!

Yes, what the hell since this is the trial you have to go through, sometimes, and this is the trial of the actor going through the pissing hell of unemployment, which actually, so they say, strengthens you, gives you bite, focuses your energy. Yes, I will out-act them all. I will be the

GREATEST ACTOR ON EARTH!

CHAPTER 14

The siren's poison

I went home on the 19 bus. I went home and put the kettle on since this is what I always do when I get home. A kind of meditation, a kind of ritual. Then she came home, full of little stories of the old wrecks she takes care of, and her dance class since now she has aspirations to 'modern dance' and actually she is rather good.

Sometimes I go to classes with her and stand a little way behind her at the 'barre'. Yes she is good. And she's bright, and she's fun, and she's lively, and she's humorous, and she's clever, and she's talented, and she's a great companion but we can't fuck any more. Don't know why, since we used to fuck so nicely together. Used to be incredible, lively, erotic, frizzy, electric, pash, pash, pash. But now no more. Alas. But we stick together since we love each other so much. We do stick together like we're the greatest mates in the world.

Buuuuut! I met this shag, who's a singer possessing a great wet delish pussy and we made love like beasts, but gentle beasts, and I left my cock inside her and fell asleep and she said she liked that … it was very 'husbandy'. She placed a rose on my pillow that she picked from the garden when she left in the morning, very romantic. But I still loved my wife.

Now my wife had taken a part-time course in Scotland and so was away half the week which was very convenient to see my singer. Yet the shag was getting to me via my cock, was injecting her siren's poison through my cock, and I was getting ever so slightly hooked.

AAAAAAAAAAAAAAAAAAAAAH!

Suddenly I had a girlfriend again whom I fucked which is what you're meant to do with a girlfriend since you trust each other and fuck each other, and did she love fucking and she was a great fuck, and a giving fuck, and a wholesome fuck. And I loved wetting her up and ploughing her field and she wasn't even averse to sucking … sometimes.

But I loved my wife, and wanted always to love my wife and never wanted to leave my wife, as long as I could fuck my singing shag, and this seems a normal thing to do, to have a great mate whom you grow old with and have lots of shags on the side since none of these shags have even a pinch of the qualities of my wife.

Oh how dumb they are, and how simple, and after coming how quickly I want to flee. Get out! But they are nice and I suppose you are nice for them and so it can work both ways, at least if nobody has to divorce and leave howling kids and suicidal wives and all can be happy — but the bitches want it all. Oh yes, how they don't give a damn about ripping your relationship apart. What vicious bitches they can be.

What a bitch she was, and the wife came back from Scotland, but I was moody, missing the bitch that had contaminated me with her cunt, and fucked with my head, and I was missing her and my wife saw me being moody but I held it back. You see the bitch said that she wouldn't see me anymore unless I left my wife! And it was v. painful and the bitch didn't like me just to fuck her and leave to go home and begged me to stay the night and god it was so very hard, so very painful, so awful. I felt like a lying and betraying beast hooked on heroin and had to go to get my 'fix'. But in the morning, I couldn't wait to rush home and reassure my darling and beloved wife that this was all an aberration and that soon I would get over it and purge her from my system and I did try, yes, I did try. I tried so hard because though I desired my shag badly at times, I loved my wife. I didn't love the shag but needed the shag. Damn it. Pulled apart...

I HATE THAT FEELING OF BEING PULLED APART.

My wife went back to complete the course in Edinburgh so then I had freedom! Then just when I had so much freedom to see the shagging hag who had captured me she gave me an ultimatum. She would give me a month off. In other words, she wouldn't see me for a month to let me make a decision, to deal with my wife and settle it since she didn't want to be shared, and it was summer and the days were bright and long, and the parks filled with lovers and I was so, so horribly alone, horribly alone as I had never been and had no one, not my wife and not my bitch and so was without nourishment or comfort and had to wait and wait. So I wrote to her almost each day pleading my love. This was the desired effect — to make a man go crazy, to poison his soul and heart.

My darling wife solved things in her own way by having an affair of her own and getting well and truly pregnant by a sleazy dancer from Poland who couldn't give a fuck about her! So now I was well and truly lumbered since my wife made visits back to London and needed to be back with me but I was truly in lovey-dove now with my shag singer and yet felt extreme pain for my wife. Ah well. She asked me if she should get an abortion since we had one a year or two before which was a big shame, and so I said, no, absolutely NO! That she would regret it and she's getting older and we would work it out somehow ... it would work itself out somehow since these things do have a way of working themselves out. Since it's a positive step, and you're bringing life into the world.

So she went back to Scotland and I carried on seeing my tits and arse. I enjoyed seeing her even if her mates were all like low class pop musicians and she always wanted to go to see low class dumb acts at clubs. At least I could escape, but now I was on probation and I was getting sick with the missing and still writing these effusive letters since I was going out of my mind.

My only relief was writing, and writing these romantic letters in which I distilled every passion and feeling I had for her, for love, for sorrow, for missing, for needing, for wanting, and it all poured out of me. And it came to pass, oh yes, it came to pass that one day I tried writing a play and the letters became the backbone of the play and the plot was woven around an old plot derived from some old classic, but my letters became the dialogue between the lovers and one day I did put the play on and it worked. Oh yes, it did work after much hassle from the actors. And the play was a mini hit!! And suddenly I became minifamous and everybody loved the play and the passion and the loving and the sexual needing and pleading and wanting and desiring ... and so all the suffering that I was put through I was able to redirect.

But one day the bitch eventually left me. I had fulfilled all that she desired and much of what I desired, it was very painful at first — an unbelievable wrench — but suddenly I felt liberated. And what a favour she did me really, since after a while she became a nagging needing pain in the bum. Like they all do when they get a mug who loves them and then they ask for money continually, and then one day she hopped off to the USA! Well done.

I did miss her a tad at first and was painfully lonely again, yet again! But now I am with my nice nurse who now has desires to be a dancer and she looks after my cats which is one of the reasons I allowed her into my house, for the cats, cause the cats liked her. Yes!

The play went nowhere else and soon it was forgotten about and no cunt from the major theatres took any interest cause basically they're emotionally retarded runts, particularly one greasy slob, or maybe two or three. Slobs, who run big companies and put on shit continuously.

So Saturday came round again, time for my workshop and I walked up the stairs with a jubilant hop and again we stared at each other, again did some exercises, some of which I took, and the feeling was that we were getting a little more focused as a group. We were getting into the swing a little more and I did a piece of O'Neill and others did their bits, and we all criticised each other – positively of course.

Actors are strangely vacant as a group, like they don't know what to do or what roles to study, or have any system to follow so that they just sit there and wait for some exercises or get up to do their piece. So we decided that we must do 'scenes' since that is what acting is ... 'reacting' to others, being provoked, stimulated, listening, responding. And that took time to work out.

Singers know immediately. They would have at least 50 arias at their disposal, and dancers would have their exercises. However, no art form is so brutalised as the actor's craft, so vitiated, corrupted by TV soaps and ads and movies, so much so that any simple tart model feels she can study it and learn some lines. That's all she can do, the simpering model tart who feels it's just about having a pretty vacant face and a fuckable body that drives men wild. They are artless chumps, just idiots, and when they do get on the stage and some of them are actually tempted to do this, they actually feel they can do it without some manager screaming

NO, NO, NO.

Don't throw your career away. And then we have the movie stars who suddenly feel tempted to dip the toe into the shark infested pool of 'live' theatre. Think it will validate them – and of course they get whacked by the critics, they really get beaten up, and then they crawl back to Hollywood and their big trailers with their tail between their legs! Fuck em! Big fucking trailer-trash earning millions and giving us zilch, but the same idiot voice and face.

― ― ―

CHAPTER 15

The emotional skin trade

―――――

So what, and now is now and there's a new bitch on the side who wants more than the afternoon bunk up or the long wait between the coast being clear while my home bitch goes off for a couple of days. Now it's been a long time and I'm as horny as a box of rabbits and I need her

DESPERATELY!

It's horrible and marvellous, this terrible yearning, this full fronted desire and when you're unemployed it gets worse and she won't see me unless I take her out at night. Which is a problem since I hate lying and covering up, and so why even live with another soul? But you can't live alone all your life just to fit a few bunk ups in, but did I make some hell of a great mistake, and what has my life been but a fucking sham? But when I could fuck my bitch on the side just any old time, just text her that my cock's coming over and she would text 'Oooh! When?', and then after the fucking, the sucking, the groping, the kissing, the exploring, the shooting, you were just so, so glad to be home and then you could enjoy home life for a couple of weeks with a calm mind until the urge came back. And what an urge, and what a joy, and life seemed no better, and could get no better.

But now the goal posts have got smaller, and they keep getting smaller, and you keep getting squeezed for just a little more, and a little more, almost like a junkie pleading, begging, crying for the next fix and that's how they get you. Yes that's how they get men to change their lives and break away and sometimes it is good but mostly it can be horrible. When it got to the breaking point and you told your wife or partner, and you actually made the move, wow! That can be awesomely wonderful, and such adventures in the skin trade are vital, but then the mistress decides to find another cock who is more convenient and without baggage and then …aaaaaaggh, the pain … yeooooow, excruciating, but on the benefit side, if you don't die at least you lose weight. So I could get into my old clothes once more, and so that was a benefit. But my health suffered terribly.

CHAPTER 16

Strength and need

So now my missus is going away for a few days but waiting for those days make them hang over me like an iron sheet, like lead, like walking around with stone boots on and gravity is ten times what it should be as you crawl through the hours, crawl through them with a prick rising and falling all day long and the yearning, and the longing and the fantasising. But then what joy after the torture and swingers who can just slag around will *never* ever feel that acute ecstasy, not like us, never like us, so I will wade, crawl through the day on my knees, crawl through broken glass ... But the day will come and I know that it will.

Even if I'm half a wreck in the meantime, I mustn't text the cow and plead for some release since this only tightens the noose around my own neck, yeah. For sure. Decide to keep cool, not panic and wait for her to call me. Now this is the paradox, that the more I need the bitch, need her like she is the last thing on earth, the last twat on earth, and I am going barmy, insane, goofy with desire for that sheath of hot flesh wrapped round me, I know that once it starts again, once I have whooshed and spurted, spritzed and sprayed, she will not leave me in peace ... but will tighten the noose, will start texting vile scrolls to me, hideous at times, and some of these scrolls are too vitriolic to even contemplate. The sum of it was that I am a filthy sexual coward, that I screw others whenever I can, or even worse that I have contaminated her with some vile sexual disease and that she has to go for a blood test. That my life is a lie and that my partner is not only evil but in collaboration with me! Also that I don't introduce her to anyone as if she was just a worthless sludge, and this is her main grudge. No doubt she is at times bitterly lonely since I don't believe she could ever have long or lasting friendships with that bitter and suspicious temperament. And that I should be giving her money, more money, much more and this is the cost, this is the payment; this is the bill after each shag.

But then you might say 'For God's sake man, give it up, get rid of it, this woman is fucking dangerous.' Yes, yes, she is dangerous, really dangerous. This is why I have such a conflict between wishing for the poisoned fruit and needing it or going cold turkey. And why not try to find someone else, a lovely tender, sweet older woman, married if possible. But as you all know you start to reach a certain age and it's too much stress to begin the hunt again. What you have to offer is usually not as reliable as it was ... as it used to be ... whereas with this one, with her it happened just so easily, without stress, without concern. Since I didn't care, either it works or not, and if it doesn't so what. And so it did simply because it didn't matter. Cocks are like that.

INFURITATING LITTLE BASTARDS.

It happened easily, pleasantly, gently and god I was happy since I thought it may not happen again.

"It's been a long time. Maybe we should just have a cuddle."

"Yes," she said, "that's better for me too. Just a cuddle, to see how we get on."

"Yes, it takes time to get used to someone."

Just a cuddle then and so I pulled off my pants and slid into bed and there was no strain and I was able to purge myself of the last vixen, the last one that crippled me and nearly drove me into insanity. For when you part and it's not resolved, you're left with a great bleeding, weeping wound, a great fucking gash. And so I plunged into my new bitch and started from that moment to heal. I almost wept with happiness.

But then, or after a while, as always seems to happen and I suppose quite naturally, she expects more and more of you and when you can't do this or can't do that, when because of your circumstances you just can't give more, then, yes, oh then doth the poison flow!

Suddenly she loosened up and started texting me the useless info of her daily insane life as if I had a vested interest in the garbage that constitutes her waking hours.

Then I thought I'd risk shooting off a bit of sexy filth about having a hard on and was stiff with desire. She kinda warmed to that but offered nothing in the way of an invite since she had it fixed in her twat that fucks were index-linked to nights out — fair enough, so they should be. But still ooh'd and aah'd when I said might have to wank thinking of her sexy wet pussy.

Silence for a while and expectations of her litany of abuse like that's all I use her for, which has been her latest mantra ... then a very warm response to the word 'wank' but still no invite. So I held on to my filthy thick cock rising and falling, rising and falling.

By now I was in real pain such as I have seldom felt before, and even thought of entertaining the idea of a massage parlour that I used to frequent in Camden. The married man's pit-stop. God, I used to go to so many, especially after I first got married. I mean our sexual life lasted about four years and then it just died a death. While it was alive it was really warm and nice and I did love her ... but my lust was put in a cage, and the door was bolted shut.

So I thought I would go in my room and do some work and learn some speeches for the next workshop, when the bitch rang and I answered and she was full of useless flannel since she is the battiest woman I have ever spent time with. And I said how much I needed to shoot my bolt and would she help me and she kept saying no, denying me, denying the need.

I begged, I wheedled, I whined. Eventually she

relented and said okay, come on over, but not for long since her kid would be home from school and she had to pick him up, which suited me perfectly and so I did but her period had just started. The world was against me! She didn't want to fuck and so I aided myself with a bit of saliva but not too much since my mouth was bone dry for some reason, probably too much anticipation. And so we talked about arses, cocks, spunk, mouths, and so a sliver of cream gratefully spat out of my cock and what a

BLOODY RELIEF!

And now as all men will concur when you're with your shag, the moments after an orgasm and before you can get out of her house are the longest in the world. I rushed to the bathroom and cleaned my flaccid tube and felt so fucking relaxed. Oh god yes!

Oh yes, that's so much better and thank you Lord for constructing us this way so we don't have a need to linger around but just get the fuck out of there before another predator bites our arse, since I am sure that is the biological reason for this escape or die imperative. Not because I'm selfish and self-absorbed. So now I was relaxed, said we'd speak later and got out of there and went for a long walk ...oh, oh, oh so important to lose

SPUNK!

CHAPTER 17

Magic of my art

―――――

So Sunday came round again but still relaxed from m recent explosion, and the wife was back and we took ourselves for a walk round Covent Garden which was once a wonderful, tangled mess of streets and alleyways – second-hand bookshops and small cafés, now turned into yet another ghastly cesspit of multiple brand stores.

However there are just a few pockets of what one might call

REAL LIFE

and the Monmouth Coffee House is still there with exactly the same heavy polished wooden tables and seats as it was when I first went there thirty years ago. So something survives.

And as if to deodorise the over-portent sense of consumerism, street performers are allowed to pitch for a cattle space to demonstrate their art and to humanise the place somewhat. We wandered into the square where we saw a couple of wonderful acrobat entertainers and the whole crowd was amazed at how brilliantly the body can be trained to show the most daring flights of imagination.

Then the next act was a Charlie Chaplin impersonator. I'd seen him before and had just longed to see him again and here he was, like a dream come true, like a wish fulfilled. What a joy he was, as if he had really inherited the mantle of Charlie. He was utterly faultless and soon the crowd built up again having dispersed after the acrobats. He took two children as assistants and of course nothing in the world can be more charming than children trying to enter in the fun, and doing so with absolute abandon. One thinks, where do these people come from? Where had this little man been all his life that suddenly he appears to us in Covent Garden? It made the sun shine in our hearts and all sloth, bile, rubbish, fears were falling away from us like slime, being washed away and we were made purer by his wholesome charm and invention.

So we watched and smiled and were brought back to the wonder of our childhood and the innocence of games, of trying to balance a pile of bricks to an extraordinary height. And the Brits who love to watch music hall, comedians, entertainers, were enchanted, and one or two were even brought in to help out and did so willingly.

For a few short loving minutes we were carried away, for this is what good performers do for us, they purge us, they cleanse us, they sacrifice something for us and they make us whole and clean again. Unlike the theatre where you pay fortunes and you are sickened by the trash you see and can't wait to get out, but here you pay nothing, only your little tribute at the end and there was something even a bit holy in this man since his act was imbued with such gentle observations. And at the end all the crowd started to dig in their purses and search for a little silver to give to this talented man who had made our lives better that afternoon and cleansed this part of the world from all the tyrants and killers, and murderers of the soul.

And then we went home and I was so glad I was an actor and only wished I could act more, and give more, and show more, and perform more, and make people happy and make them laugh and squeal, and how I wished to be a street performer delighting people with the unexpected, with the magic of my art, and the tricks I had learned. So we went home to our little flat in North London and she made a wonderful dinner that night and was happy to do so, since maybe a little Charlie was in the cooking?

CHAPTER 18

Work

My new agent's a bum, but then aren't they all, but at least he's a decent bum and pleasant, but they can only hoover up what you are currently worth on the market and if your stock is as low as mine is, you have to wait for the odd bits where they need someone quick or who just fits the bill after the best have been cast. If you've been in the network and have slimed up to a few of those fucking useless directors who are so full of shit and yet for some reason always lauded since the standards are rock bottom, then you might be on their little list.

And so you are like some tart waiting for the phone to ring, and you feel emasculated like a fucking tart waiting for the fucking phone to ring. So rather than be a fucking tart waiting for the fucking phone to ring I am trying to get some wanky actors to commit to the workshops so that we can create when and how we like, and thus be men, be women, and be an entity. In the meantime I am waiting for the fucking phone to ring.

He's got me a bit of work now and again but it's usually a cameo, a bit of crap at the end of a movie, and most recently I was offered a day in a movie as a walk on! A figure that appears right at the end and has one line, virtually a fucking extra! And then I did get a job in a Japanese video game to model for the creatures that we would become and that was a fun wank as we were shipped halfway across the world to some dead zone in New Zealand. The cast were nice but the place was so dull I got square eyes watching TV in the hotel room since the weather was so bad it being their winter.

My first agent was still part of the old school which had dozens of actors on their books and you could always scrape by on some rep job. He was a nice fellow and a poof, but a pleasant poof, who had himself been an actor, and I am sure didn't know what to make of me, but got me some tacky work. But he did get me started and that was good. Then I joined a new guy who was a real character and absolutely full of himself and gave a lecture on what good acting was and he got me a job in some dump rep in Dundee which was a dreary place on this side of hell, but only just on the border. After my first role, which was painfully small, I showed some spirit so the director kept me on for another dreary piece of piss, and at least I found a tart I could fuck, and that was just so important in rep where the days can be so lonely, and the nights, if you don't have a cuddle. And she was a nice cuddle, until for some reason she went off me. The director went on to do TV but was never very friendly to me although he tried in his way.

Then I got a job in Barrow in Furness, if you can believe that such places exist.

But they do, and I remember the first day getting into my digs and making friends with the cast and then doing my first Brecht play which for some reason I took to like a rat to water. Here I got lucky again with a sweet actress called Hazel, who had limpid brown eyes and a lovely body, and thank god for that. However that came later.

One night, getting up to go to the loo I noticed the landlady, a middle aged tart, creeping about. I was naked and grew a huge hard on and grabbed her and kissed her and she kissed me back hard, and I took her into my room and fucked her which was just wonderful for there is nothing in the world like an unexpected fuck. Especially a landlady. I never forgot that old bird — those ladies, like sanctuaries in the night.

I enjoyed acting the Brecht since the director encouraged freedom and I started to find myself for the first time. Good old Derek, for that was his name. Got well and truly rat-arsed on the last night and Hazel and I went out and brought back some fish and chips for such was our fare in those olden times, and so thank you, and bless you, dear darling Hazel with your beautiful hazel eyes. Heady romance!

But then there was Chesterfield with the crooked steeple which seemed to cast its warp over the whole town. It was crawling into late autumn and the days were chill and we'd all eaten bacon rolls in the little café opposite the theatre and a little mandarin of a director who looked like a cat gave me instructions on how to act the role which was stiff and unyielding, and totally blocked my progress by saying, "You'll get a laugh on this line and if not I'll want to know why!"

And so it started on a sour note and the play was a rotten old Victorian whodunnit such as is favoured in these grisly outposts. But the second play was Antigone in which I played Haemon, so I was in with a chance but it was directed by yet another self-aggrandising prick, since they seem to get everywhere in the theatre like some kind of plague, but what the hell, who else could put up with it. And he had the most peculiar manner of speech combined with an Aussie accent. But he wasn't unpleasant and we just got on with it, and there was no one to fuck and so I was lonely as hell. All I recall is that one day after rehearsal I took a long walk and within a short time found myself into the countryside, and feeling better amidst the beautiful golden cornfields, all alone and happy, and realising how much I miss of this by being in London.

I did have one romance in the last week. I can't remember anything about it except that it was so fleeting and the girl was a stage manager for a touring company that came for the night. Sometimes you just forget these things and yet I recall her being very sweet and gentle. I made friends with no-one except a stage manager who then became a mate in London for a while because we both liked and were fans of the same glorious actress/ trooper called Liz who seemed to really like young lads, which I still was at that time. She was a fabulously crazy, zany, powerful woman.

The worst time was a one off piece of shit which should have been called 'Not in my Lifetime', one of those ghastly potboilers directed, if that could possibly be the right word, by a lunatic who was the most unsavoury being I had yet come across, one of those bottom of the barrel types whose nasty productions dotted the provincial British landscapes like weeping sores.

We had one week in an unpalatable town whose name should be erased from the face of the earth. Since in those far off days you had to search for your own digs, I and one of the company spent five hours walking around the town, and there was no room at the inn, anywhere. At last we fell into a boarding house and politely requested a room, or rooms, and vegetarian breakfast and dinner for my delicate friend, since in those days they did both. The gross and belaboured old hag replied that she didn't want fussy tenants, to which we quickly responded that we weren't in the least bit fussy, since we were desperate for a room. And we were there after all.

The next sordid day we did a kind of dress rehearsal for this abomination of a play and then struggled through the evening. The morning press had at least not lost its irony when the reporter said 'he waited eagerly for the set to fall down!'. That was about all he could derive from the horror that we put on, keenness in its disaster.

God knows why but I decided to call my agent. I say God knows why since if there was something to say, he would tell me, but you do it out of habit, not because you expect him to say 'Oh by the way I've got a nice little telly for you', but just to hear some warmth in his voice, some encouragement, some how's it going, come and have a bite next week – even showing some tinge of concern or care about you helps. But he doesn't do 'compassion', my agent. I hate calling, I really hate it ... don't want to ... don't want to look or sound like a fucking unemployed bum of an actor which is unfortunately what I am or have become. Don't want to be one of those actors who are always 'checking in' and more times than not hearing some dreary voiced tart of a secretary who tells you that he is tied up at the moment and so you wait and develop a larger and larger hump on your back of guilt, the longer he takes to call you back.

Since the length of time it takes serves as a barometer of how much he cares. So, don't, but my hand crawls towards the phone and do you know what? ... it's the same knowing, numbing feeling that I get when I crave essence of bitch ...

BUT I STILL DO.

CHAPTER 19

Secret snatch

Those days are over and well and truly. That's what I tell myself. But I was able to sneak out and see the bitch again since the missus had an unexpected callout, and what a relief that was, and so after much abuse from the bitch for not seeing her or staying the night and telling me to fuck off etc fucking etc, I offered to take her out to dinner to wherever she liked, which obviously hit the spot since she is feeling neglected and doesn't get taken out too much.

And so she picked a really fancy café where the food was first class shit but the atmos was good, and my head was constantly on a potter's wheel. I even saw the Pinters, who must be very bored to go to such a place and eat such ordinary food. Now I knew the Pinters since during a slack period, not unlike now, I was a minicab driver for a quite luxurious limo company in that neck of the woods and was often 'requested' by them. So I shunted shyly over and passed some compliments on his health since he looked quite good and he didn't have a fuck's clue who I was, but she was pleasant and asked me where I got my fancy belt, and then I slinked proudly back to my table.

And after, the fucking was quite wonderful, since I had such a need for her and she is such a horny bitchy steamy runt and thin and full of fuck, and I thought I would stay the night for a change.

But as soon as I came I wanted to get the hell out of there with the same intensity as I wished to be there in the first place, like it was and is the only place in the world I want to be, and that nothing in life can compare – at least until I want to leave again. After I just wish to escape and feel so fulfilled and free and liberated since we are made differently and have to deal with our biological differences. Or rather she does. I mean she's ready for the next mate to mount her, and then may the best sperm win. At least, that's how it was and now we have to learn to be civilised and loving and fight against our natural desires. But it was wonderful.

Only, the downside is that after a few days she starts nagging to see me again. Not on. It takes me a few days to recover after all. I'm not a young kid anymore. She not only nags but abuses in the vilest way since she is clearly a scrubber. When you are married or living a deux and need something on the side you're rarely going to get first class fillet, but old bits, cut off the bone, scraggy, half mental. For the smart women, the beauties, rarely wish to go out with a man who's answered for, but the scrubbers don't give a damn and just want some cock and a free meal and occasional hand-out, and then they're begging you to get rid of the woman you love more than anything in the world, but whose pussy no longer exists for you. So it's a dilemma, since after the fuck I only want to be with my beloved lady but I can't take the lunatic messages anymore so I should cut out. Then after a few weeks I begin to grow slightly crazy, and endure the terrible prospect of

COLD TURKEY.

The trouble with secret snatch is that it tends to cast a shadow over the rest of your activities. I like to call her when I suddenly have free time, leap over there and dive into bed. She seems to have as much hunger for me as I do for her and it's like a hunger that you need to fulfil immediately. If she's busy and I have to wait a few days, it seems to clog my mind and I can't plan anything else in the interim, can't concentrate on seeing a friend or friends since my mind is half out-of-joint, thinking about the moment when I get replugged in.

Some men or women can do both. Lead fruitful and eventful lives and the syrup on the side has no effect, but for some reason it does affect me. It insinuates itself into a corner of my mind like a cockroach nibbling away in the attic. The drug changes your metabolism and it is worse if it's too long ahead as I can't even look at my wife properly for that period. As if my eyes were mini

TV monitors into which she could see the filthy images in my brain. So when I want to see the bitch it has to be now, right now, when I call. I'm free now and if not now maybe in an hour or two or three but no more.

No, I can't live with a secret ... with a secret hanging over my head ... can't sit in my home. Sit at the table with my beautiful wife and eat her lovely food and know how much time she has taken over it, how much time she spent shopping for it. Going to the same boring tedious supermarket and coming home laden with heavy bags and looking forward to creating a lovely meal since those days are the best when we were together and free, not now. Not when the gnawing 'roach is in my skull' and then she can tell. I know she can tell, cause I'm suddenly too polite, too concerned ... to try to find something to talk about.

My natural spontaneity goes, my jokey anarchic humour goes ... I'm not unpredictable. I'm soggy and so I'm glad when dinner is over. Glad, so glad, when what should be the most enjoyable part of my day is over.

You can switch off; you need to do something to get your mind off it. I'd go to a matinee. That's what I do sometimes, just take myself to a matinee. A seat behind a pillar rendered a ticket cheap enough to take in the latest Osborne revival. Being a matinee, and revival, I trundled along alone and took my seat, and truly enough it was in the fine old tradition of dull British theatre. So I wasn't too disappointed, just lowered any expectations, took an occasional nap and saw it through. Being a long way back didn't help too much so I must get new glasses and not lose them this time.

'The Entertainer' is now a very limited play endlessly repeating the same dogged theme of nasty Mr England, drunk deadbeat dad bringing shags home (impossible to believe), a family ill-thrown together, old England epitomised in the granddad and everybody behaving according to the dull dreary rules. At least Olivier made it somewhat glorious and enchanted you with his skills, tap dancing on the stage. The actor I was watching had limited music hall skills and what he used didn't really convince although he had a brave go, but that's not enough. Olivier commented on the music hall world while this guy tried to be it. The room was awful and dead where the family lived. They're not in prison but in a typical working class flat, and all they did was drink. Too sour. Far too sour. The simple Brit audience went along with it as they do and I was so glad when it ended.

The great thing about theatre is the relief you get when you come out.

After, I met an old mate and he took me to dinner in Joe Allen, which is still one of the friendliest cafés in London, and we had a really good chatter which we always do and a couple of full bodied glasses of plonk and then I crashed out, peaceable and easily, to

DREAM.

Dreamt that I saw two of my old mates who died recently

return from the dead. They looked fresher and clear skinned although pale and I asked what they were doing here, and were they kind of giving me a hint? And I said "am I going next week or so?" Although I didn't know why I said this, except that since they were there it couldn't be that far away. And one of them, Bill, said, "Maybe…"

Then I dreamt of some young, lovely, pretty woman. We were together and suddenly cuddling under the sheets and she put her hand on my cock. I had my knickers on, and though I desired her madly, she was so sweetly lovely, I knew I had to take my time, before my confidence was at full swing.

Then I saw young people doing jumps from high walls and I recall how I too used to do that in my dreams, when I was on top of a high wall and there was no place to go but down, and when I jumped I felt no pain, nor hurt.

END OF DREAM.

CHAPTER 20

Star

So Olivier was born a hundred years ago! Well, nobody has replaced him, nor are they likely to, since what he did was to do it himself and not wait for some drip to offer him a little go at something. He started up his own team of actors and that made him a man, and a leader, and at the same time that gives a man strength. The best have always done it alone, generating their own ideas and desires. Some have been hired hands and have also reached the pinnacle but that is the exception rather than the rule.

Tired as hell today, so shall give it a rest. Not much going on, just drifting and can't seem to get the machine working. I had a dream that one day I would be a great actor. Standing on the large stages of the world, and astounding the audience with my brilliance. Being asked to perform my Macbeth, Hamlet, Othello. Creating great works of astounding plays, directing them with flair, innovation such as are rarely, if ever seen. Doing my Cyrano, Richard III, Oberon, in fantastically created productions. And after, sweat pouring off me in my dressing room as I wait for my beautiful woman to come backstage, bulging with pride and smiles, pouring the champagne, and then going for an elegant dinner in one of those rich, star-studded restaurants where you are greeted like you're the king of the business and people are waving to you from distant tables. Flying above the mob as the adrenalin pours through you. Respected, adored, lionised, with reviews acclaiming you as the king of beasts.

OH YEAH!

CHAPTER 21

Bump and grind

It has come to this ... my cock is suddenly on fire and totally obsessed with grinding it into the one bitch who is the Satan, but I need it so much I can't get it out of my mind. And yet I have to find a ploy, a device, an excuse, and I am such a bad liar and on weekends it is even more difficult, but the hours crawl by and I can barely talk to my partner but make occasional grunts and meanwhile forget everything, but can't just hang around the house anymore and so invent a friend and arrange to have a meeting. It's been okayish lately since a hot spunking can last me for weeks, but now I have the bitch on my mind and my mind is not open and clear so I want to get rid of her. Then the deep gnawing urges like a ravenous rat chewing away sweetly at my vitals. I think just go to the gym and get rid of all

SICKENING DESIRE.

But I did it. With a little courage I lied about a meeting with an old friend and slipped out and waves of freedom flew past my ears as my car wound its way into the entrails of London's byways, finding itself at last in a rundown street whose houses faced the railway tracks. I rang the bell and the kid let me in. The place was as usual a grubby mess of clothes, papers, books, junk, old toys, worn out and depressed. A rabbit was tearing up bits of newspaper in its cage and the small hallway was stuffed with boxes of more junk and mess so that you had to walk over it.

She put on the kettle but wanted to go out for lunch with the kid which was the usual 'fee' or ritual before we got down to the act. However she agreed to a little messing in the filthy bedroom before going and so I lay on the bed and had my cock out and eager in no time and it felt good to be out and free. My cock was thick and anticipating it, the gorging of a big juicy feast. She had to whip out her Tampax that she had just put in since she was still able to 'mens', but then she slid down on my cock and all felt good again, even on that grubby bed in that filthy room. She didn't want me to come just yet, leaving the reward for after I had done my duty and taken them both out.

So we got in the car and I was timing how long I could get away with seeing my 'friend', so we drove into Kensington heading for the nice Med café where we had enjoyed a few snacks in the past but it was full, being a rare sunny day, and so we went to the gastro pub next door. Being England there was no service and you had to go inside to order at the bar, although you wouldn't have known it and could have sat there for ever Waiting For Godot, and so I went inside and an idiot orang-utan merely nodded as her way of saying 'What the fuck do you want', and so I asked politely if she could speak, to which she replied haughtily ... "Of course I can speak."

I then ordered the food which she got wrong and then had to wait till she cancelled the first order and went through the rigmarole of refunding my money. I then had to go in and out three times to ask the sullen bitch if somebody could clean our table, which did eventually happen, but this is England and therefore the usual conduct for pubs. Even if they have advanced to gastro status the slob British gene is still wriggling healthily in their DNA.

However the food came and was just about ok and we all enjoyed slurping down our grub and chatting happily about British slob life, which was also her particular forte since she always had insane stories of how her brilliant son was always being castigated by callous and insensitive teachers and her favourite drink was 'whine'.

Then we drove back and swiftly got into bed and it felt really nice and she did the usual which was good and got on my cock and worked away and I exploded inside her, washed off in the grotty bathroom, sipped some tea, slipped her a prezzie and then fled as soon as I could, feeling liberated. Thank god.

But it's the aftermath — the calls, the endless messages,

and the veiled threats. The hints that I might have given her some unknown disease since she always accused me of sleeping around and of not asking her out to meet people as if I was a free agent, which I am not since I love my partner, and how can I introduce her to anyone who would know my wife. But insane bitches have no sense of reality. I had put up with the filthy abuse for a long time and now I want out, out, out please!

But still the messages come, first suggesting that I might have infected her and then 'I luv u' messages in which she pretends to her vile self that in some insane universe I love her! Cunt is drug and the more she abused me the more I needed cunt but now must cut out since insanity has no borders, it's a limitless world. Beware.

BEWARE!

These people will suck not only your cock but your will, your power, your sanity and your life. Fine while it lasted, very fine and first rate fucking (allowing for my own limitations), but fine and full scores on that mark. But this time her messages were so whiny, so pitifully complaining, that I wished her out of my life and she looked awful since she is sick with something, is thin as a whip and as white as a sheet, and her grey hair is growing out of its blond camouflage and she looks like a witch. Although it did thankfully get me over the other mad, insane bitch I had before.

Shall take it easy for a while and not brood but get on

with my workshop and I now have a pretty decent group of actors who are enjoying the once weekly workouts. Now we must find a theme! So I thought why not do a good old pot boiler like Macbeth? I fancy this quite a lot. We will make it really funky, sexy, violent and most of all

EXCITING.

CHAPTER 22

A matter of life and death

Oh, oh, oh! The shit has hit the fan. As it so often does with evil bitches who seem to comprise over one half of the entire female gender. I have been assaulted by the fiend. After our last encounter she once more started on her old theme of contamination and then the pleading for money to go to 'alternative therapy', plus other unsavoury little subplots and filthy accusations and insults about my partner until I had to send her a message to stop or I'll call the police on her, which did at least curtail her wilder spewing of filth.

Then the days and weeks passed and I heard little and all was at peace. However I felt the raging horn of lust begin to trumpet and my mind wandered to the picture gallery in my brain and desire once more sneaked into my bones. I was ignoring her little pleas for company and tales of her rabbit dying, when her tears over the phone felt like the oozing of pus from a leper, particularly as the message came so soon after one of her more abusive tirades. And when I'm with my real old lady I don't like to be in contact with the fiend so that I can be at peace and just enjoy the tranquil evenings and our occasional dinners out.

So now the old bird has gone away and this usually was the time for me to frolic a bit and have some carnal delights, like having my cock sucked while she wanked which was utterly delicious, and she seemed to enjoy it enormously so that in the seamy sheets we had a lovely sweaty horny filthy old time, even if the flat was like a squalid dump, a piss hole like I had never before seen. Sometimes I feared for my health on that bug ridden sofa upon whose stains she had put a fancy cover. And there she would just descend upon my cock which was the best feeling in the world. Just descend upon it, pulling her knickers to one side without much ado. Then we'd go into the bedroom and continue for some time. Her tits were worn out old dugs but then I'm not too fussy since the legs were very good and she was thin with a nice arse. Her hair was long and thick and dyed to cover silver grey which kept growing out and so she reminded me of nothing so much as a witchy hag. She was forever whining about the neighbours, her son's teachers, and the other kids — like the entire world was in a conspiracy against the creature, while in fact

SHE

was the most evil beast I had ever come across. But whether my own gentle nature thrived on abuse I cannot say but I kept going back to the filthy hag and begging for pussy since her engine was oily and silky smooth and tight, and so one shut one's eyes to the grubby muck and rubbish everywhere, and empty boxes and everything on the floor including two giant stuffed giraffe toys which you had to keep stepping over to get to the bathroom to wash my cock after I'd lubricated her flute.

Took a break for a while as lots of things happened, one of which was my sister dying. I had thought about that for a long time, and to be truthful, I had no feeling about her whatsoever. But when I went to see her in the coffin I was much moved to tell her how much I loved her since we did know each other for bunches of years. Yet towards the end she had got a strange habit of being sarcastic and nasty to me and I began to not only resent her but actually loathe the sight and sound of her. But now the poor cow is dead and so the memories of our youth came back and I felt a huge and overwhelming sadness for this dead body in front of me and I touched her face which was cold and stiff, but her stomach was still soft since I gently pressed it. She was so thin that I hardly recognised her, poor beast. How she must have suffered towards the end. Never able to eat, but at least she did have her only child to look after her. So now that's over! Now they're all dead except for me, the last one, and of course a few cousins waddling about.

And then my cousin Kitty died suddenly and there was another funeral to go to, and I saw the cousins and made inane chat with them, and this time it was in a beautiful cemetery with trees and flowers and not those ghastly pared down puritanical Jewish graveyards. I saw my sister's son there and he seemed to be ok and he is an actor like his uncle so I must have influenced him somewhat, but though he makes money he doesn't seem to be too successful, even though he is not without talent.

Still no work coming in from my stinking agent and I don't care too much since we're getting this workshop going and I know that this will make something happen that is mine, and that will be lasting, and not just a bit of dosh and some per diem and a rotted brain. I now have actors coming on a regular basis.

Much in the paper about the scumbags who pay no tax or very little, getting away with offshore scams. And nobody does anything to remedy the situation. And the Health Service can't afford high tech drugs for cancer. But what does it matter when there are D-list celebs in the papers on a daily basis and all for doing absolutely fuck all, and yet, day after fucking day, like we're all just hanging onto their coat tails for one more whiff of their smelly evacuations. What do they think we are, this servile, dumb, British public, ready to soak up the last dribbles of celebrity slime. Day after day, she is there, he is here, she is going there, they're both going here – and following like a great greasy turd is the press.

　　Life goes on.

CHAPTER 23

Blow thy horn

———

My horn's been a bit tricky lately since my old lady is back. Have to not only be careful, but wish to be careful, and not only enjoy the woman I am with but protect our relationship since the other is the spawn of Satan. A horrible clinging piece of sleaze, that won't stay away and keeps up the pretence that I'm her lover even when I don't respond to her endless messages. The Satan is dangerous and one does not know what the devil is capable of, one doesn't know what this lump of foul deformity could do.

When the time comes, when the spunk builds up and the temptation comes, then I must be strong and get rid of it elsewhere. In my younger days it might have been a massage parlour, which this city is bountiful in, and some were not bad, and in some I did have, or was given, the most delicious wanks and so these nice ladies have served me in fact all over the world, and rarely have I been dissatisfied. I recall one of the first ones I went to near Amhurst Park, on the way to Mum's for my Friday night supper (which I used to look forward to), and I noticed this little light of temptation with 'Massage' in lights written above the door. And lo and behold, my tool was as hard and stiff as it could get, and this delicious woman was oiling and stroking my shaft and I had her lovely tit in my mouth and in those days I came like a rocket, if you'll forgive the expression. And I went back there a few times and was totally zapped out each time. These were sublime outlets for men who can no longer fuck their wives, and yet don't really wish to leave their wives either, since once the cock is made dormant your wife is everything you could wish for. Or nearly.

Then there was a place in Camden Town which was a bit sleazy but ok and you had a little bit of a choice since the purveyors of relief would sit lined up and then you made a choice, and much spunk has flowed through Camden Town. I also went to a place just off Kings Cross trying it out for the first time and the bloke in charge, who I didn't like, made me wait and then sent in a nice middle aged bird. It might have been the first time since she was rather demure and uncertain, but she soon got to work and gave me a touch of anal tickling which really put me into orbit and I went wild with joy, and after he asked if she was ok, and I said "Hey, absolutely."

So this went on for quite a few years and I became a bit of an expert, so to speak, on the joys of London saunas, which were anything but a sauna, but quite pleasant therapy centres since you didn't fuck. You just lay there, turned over and got pampered and stroked, and some were really good wankers. Absolutely first class.

Well several weeks passed after the slag's last disgusting outburst and I felt very much like sinking into that witch's sewer once more ... and so I rang but she was offhand and cold and told me to get lost more or less. I had asked her out to supper and she gave me a heap of swill and piss on the phone and so I asked someone else.

And then she rang saying where is supper, so I said that based on her last venomous call I had gone elsewhere ... that was it. A few days later I still needed her pretty bad and offered her money for some sex since I usually gave her some pocket money each time. What does she do, but call the police saying I am harassing her! So a copper rang and asked me to go to the police station in Notting Hill!

Jesus, I thought, what a filthy evil fucking menace since I had also left a message of goodwill when she didn't respond and I guessed that she had landed another pliable cock, as she is never that independent and is always blagging money. I went down there and got it sorted and half expected a mob of press there since she is not above doing that. The twisted evil cow spoke to a reporter once before since she only mixes with the shit of the world ... but she was a wonderful whore and this I loved her for, and repaid me when my horn was anxious and made it hard and did delicious naughty things which I adored and now I have lost my whore bitch!

There will be more ... please god there will be more.

And then I started to think that maybe I was a bit of a sex addict that I could listen to this filthy bitch insulting me, and even my partner whom she doesn't know, and I still go back for cunt, for what is a man without cunt ...

A BEAST, NO MORE!

Or he is without it. And then you've got to start all over again and prove yourself again, but now I am anxious with new bitches and can see myself being alone and maybe that is ok too.

The cops were at least very pleasant and didn't come out with any bullying tactics and even seemed to be a bit on my side and confided that they thought she was slightly in orbit, and advised me to steer clear which I had known about for a long while, but through my sex addiction had chosen to ignore. But what you know may be ultimately bad for you, you chase if the rewards are intense. So I left the cop house in some relief if not with a springy step, and there were no thuggish press there to greet me, since she no doubt knew that the shit flies both ways.

But it did leave me with an empty feeling. Knowing that my cock really fuels my entire being and knowing that I have to now go cold turkey was not the nicest sensation I have ever had. So what to do? Am I officially an

ADDICT?

Well I checked through the ads for massage and the like in a mag, and came across one with a 'mature' woman, which had me thinking about forties and sophisticated and svelte. She seemed pleasant on the phone, not this hard bitch voice others had. Of course when I got there, somewhere near Lancaster Gate, the door was opened by a hag easily in her sixties ... oh dear. I have been there before, haven't I just. And she was wearing a 'sexy outfit' which made her loathsomeness all the more intense. However I got in and moved to the bedroom and was pleased see that at least it was clean and not the filthy slum I had been used to with my 'lover'.

I sat in a chair and she garbled on for a while, and then I took my stuff off and lay resignedly on the bed over a towel that she had just brought in. I buried my head in the pillow and just wished for oblivion. So she touched me, rubbing a spritz of oil on my back and giving me a halfway-house massage. When she got down to my thighs I started to heat up a bit putting her old hag face out of my mind ... and then she tickled me under the balls and it started to improve and my cock stood up. Miracle! So she said turn over, and I did but kept my face well away from the old continental hag. Then she sprayed a few more drops on me and eventually came to my cock which was rock hard by this time and then she stroked it and I said I liked that and she added a bit more oil and stuck her finger in my arse, which felt quite pleasant since she wanked me at the same time.

I was enjoying it but suddenly I didn't like her hands

anymore and the whole deal started to collapse along with my cock and she pumped away but now it was all a bit frantic and my cock lost its structure somewhat and was like a baguette without the yeast. If you want a job done ... so I took over myself while she squeezed my balls and reached a half-hearted cum.

So this is what it has come to ... oh, how miserable! How sad, how forlorn, and pathetic to be without that, that which I had taken for granted my entire life ... the divine sweetness of a lover. So I paid her and left and she chatted and was pleasant and I felt a tad relieved, but sour inside, and determined never to do this again.

EVER!

CHAPTER 24

Working on the WANT

So Tony Blair is on his way out and this heavyweight slob is shuntering in to take his place like an old rusty truck. He doesn't even sound vaguely human, poor bloke. Like a computer uttering sound bites and remembering to grin reflexively every few minutes. Now suddenly the nation is waking up a bit to the scams going on in this tax haven of ours. Of course the poor prat does nothing nor does he even address it, the filthy old wanker, but raids the pension funds instead. Ever politic in politics.

It's now quite a few weeks since I had a sniff of minge, a couple of months, and it's not a good feeling. Whereas once you could take a few weeks off knowing that the bitch was there almost any time you rang, now it might just never happen again, and you gaze longingly at a couple walking together, pausing for little lip nibbles and hugs and how your heart imagines some married woman craving some sexy affection. It's not good, but I'm getting used to it just about, and maybe it's an addiction that I can freeze out of my being. I now enjoyed my dinner with my partner, actually relished it, and my cock is getting used to being silent although I don't want to lose it through neglect. But a bit of neglect after thirty years of shagging won't hurt me. And then I will place all my energies in searching for actors for my workshop and plays. Yes, get on with that

TODAY.

In my initial weakness, in the moments after the horrible realisation that the ugly bitch would no longer be sliding down my cock, no longer sit on it, pulling her knickers to one side like a randy school girl, no longer be sucking it so gently while fingering herself, I felt a deep sense of loss, but that was the evil bitch's own fault for sending me the worst, the vilest messages I ever heard. So vile I can't even write them down. But a weak man, an addicted man, will put up with any shit so long as there's a shag at the end and that prickly, ecstatic moment of spurt. I miss that moment desperately and she was a real pro and knew how to handle a man's cock like no one else I ever encountered.

At times wonderful, and the most wonderful was to go away together and know that at night you would be shagging. At night the sweetest part of your being was alive and everything else fitted in during the day just to get you to the sweet, sweet night. But that all had to end. They all have to end.

Once the urge was on me so I went out at about five in the morning cause I knew a place in the East End where a couple of birds hung out and offered blow jobs for twenty quid. I mean, they were slags, but the temptation was strong. I saw a cop car sliding around the streets and it wouldn't be hard to imagine being set up. No it wouldn't be hard to see that, and in the middle of a blow job a light shines through the window and you are nabbed! And you can bet your life that it's all a set up and the bitches are in with the law. At least some of them. And then your mug in the paper, like that actor mug in L.A.

So I circled around and fantasised about making friends with one of those brass and being nice to her until I got used to her and then could book it whenever I fancied a blow job without the necessity of long-winded relationships with their threats, abuse, whines and constant begging. It was night and I stopped, and she looked in and I wound down the window, and she said 'Twenty', and I said 'Where?', and she said 'In the car', and I said I would be back, didn't want to risk it and drove home ... safe and sound. Hmmmm. I went back to my empty bed and thought about the young woman but my cock felt quiet and I could imagine her getting in the car and being unable to even grow my tail, what with the stress and fear of being caught.

So now my missus is back and we do our separate things and wait for the evening when we can enjoy our dinner together with ample wine, and then the telly ... and then the telly ... and then the telly ... and then I climb into my bed and she kisses me goodnight with affection since there is no filth under the sheets, and I feel I must confess, a little bit

DEAD.

So I shall make an effort today to smoke less and find some actors to work on this new play, a new play that I have actually written and when I get the actors for this new play then everything will fall into place again. Who knows, I might find a little bit of excitement once again? That sliver of silky passion, that anticipation, that ever-twitching horn waiting to be fed and watered once again. But for now it's empty, dead, like a flower not watered ... it just dies, wilts, curls up ... growing older. Who will desire me again, and pant for me to wank over her? They're gone, all of them, vanished, removed, but there ought to be one around, one left, some delicious 45- year old who's craving a bit of company. I need one without all the threats, and bullying, and abuse ... without that please!

Had enough of all their bullying tactics, so now do without and actually feel a little healthier, if not clearer, and without all the sneaking, and hiding, and planning and fear whenever the phone rang! The last was a particularly evil bitch but out of all my experiences it's the evil ones who are the best, the sexiest, the most delicious, the fuckiest, the suckiest, the horniest ... something delicious in their rampant dirtiness ... delicious and delightful like a bag of sweets , sugar sweets and scrumptious.

CHAPTER 25

War and peace workshop

So the weekend sped past in a welter of nothingness and space but it was pleasant in a cotton wool sort of way, like I got up and fed the cats, and made some tea really early and rolled a fag, and got the morning paper and read it in bed, which is always the best time and after, if I feel like it, I have a bath which always bucks me up and makes me feel renewed again. Then I go to the fridge and take out some frozen peas and pop them in a pot with some olive oil and tomato puree and odd bits and bobs until I have made quite an ambitious veggie dish which is ten times better than any fry up, and read the papers which is usually just crammed full of shit and tossers' opinions on anything but not really telling you what the hell is going on. And then the back pages, sometimes nearly half of the paper, stacked full, chock full, crammed full of the biggest pile of shit called

SPORTS

as if the whole nation really had nothing much else to think about. So it doesn't take too long to get through the rotten papers and always in the sluicy bits one sees cropping up again and again like some incurable form of herpes, a lovely reality TV star or other, as if they have done something, achieved something, made something, instead of not only achieving less than nothing, minus anything, but is a great sucking hole that sucks the space out of the papers, that sucks your interest into a great vapid vacuum, that gives you nothing but an endless black hole, a warp, and yet they are in the papers everyday like a kind of goddess or god or something, some kind of being, an entity, an achiever of great things, an expresser of great talent instead of a pit of nothingness along with the garbage they attract. And we are made to read this, we are invited to partake, to look on enviously at their vapid crawling in the gutter with their scum sucking lovers, and all this is reported each day as if this was so very important to our welfare.

However, they may be very pleasant people. Sometimes I think they are merely victims of sorts, being trapped on the web by the malodorous fat slugs that employ them to push their inventive wares. The great slugs, the great spiders, sitting in the middle of the media web sucking all that come within it. Huge, dark, ugly spiders with legs spun out to catch all the innocent shoppers to the garbage pit stores. Too many spiders.

However, now I was at peace, for the day hath come when the workshop is active and I walked with a jaunty stride along Islington's Upper Street, slid into Camden Passage and up the stairs of this filthy grotty pub, and in the room where a few of the actors were warming up in that vague way that actors do who have no real or basic training. So they all scrabble about the floor doing some half-baked exercises they picked up and try to recall from drama school, and some of them doing bits of T'ai Chi, and when I get in they all gradually get up or slump into chairs and wait for me to try and focus on what the hell I am going to inspire them with.

"So, Helen, have you got that piece from Agamemnon where Clytemnestra tells the story of how she knew the Trojan wars were over by the fires that were lit on all the islands across the Aegean ... Great, yes, that's great. Good and who else?"

Terry speaks up. "Well I wouldn't mind having a go at Cyrano when he talks about his nose..."

"Oh, the great nose speech ... good, and anyone else?"

A few mumbled that they hadn't yet learned anything but would by the next time out, and that they were busy and working late shifts in the café, or the office, or had the flu and other wonky excuses that losers always have at their fingertips.

"Well" said I, "I wouldn't mind having a go myself at a piece from Macbeth."

Which is always awkward, both taking the class and at the same time wanting to participate and get that buzz when you expose your inner self. I didn't just want to be there as a mother figure patting them on the head. So it's an awkward place to be, both taking the bloody group and being the mum and dad and encouraging and criticising, and then turning into a little, needy, wanky actor who seeks approval from other little wanky actors.

So Helen went into her shtick and bloody hell, she was amazing and pulled out this great voice from somewhere and her gestures were fluid and powerful at the same time and little would I have guessed that she had this beast of a woman in her.

After all this is what acting is about. You're allowed to show your real you. Who you really are underneath all the self-denigrating and insecure shit. Underneath and flowing within us are all these turbulent rivers, all these passions, desires and heroic impulses and we really are greater, much more powerful than we allow ourselves to believe. As if, within us, stirring in some fetid pit of stagnation are multiple personalities – writhing helplessly, wanting to escape and then, suddenly they are given an exit and they come out, whooping and screaming, dancing and leaping with delight and how wonderful can that be? How purging is that? That you allow these demons a place in the sun. Also how cleansing and what relief – what sheer relief after as if you had given birth. What director can ever feel that? No, never that, but they do feel other things, the power of bringing worlds to life of giving vent to their vision, and controlling it, yes always a

CONTROL.

So we were all silent at the end of Helen's dynamic flow, and then gave her quite a round of applause and she flushed and thanked us. And then we all took the speech to bits but not without congratulating her on her extraordinary bravery and vocal power that we never once suspected she possessed and she even seemed to grow, for at the end of the speech her features seemed even more sculptured and gaunt, her eyes dark and piercing, as if she had touched that secret font of energy that we all have deep within us.

And we were suddenly all a bit envious after we had given her praise and made our little comments, which were the usual little barbs, like some of it was a tad too fast, or may be too loud at times, but all praised since we were a group and she was one of the family and she had even pulled us together, since there would be nowhere else where she could have shown this. And she confessed that she was so nervous she was almost pissing herself and we all smiled benignly and suddenly I felt a touch of compassion for the poor man who was to follow with his Cyrano. She had made us feel that we were now a serious group of actors and that she had sacrificed a part of her valuable being to us.

Terry began his speech. He came to the centre of the room and then suddenly backed away as if to let his words spring out before him. He was a good looking young man, with a fantastic voice but with little confidence, however to be sure it was slowly growing. He had this apologetic air that he carried with him and even grinned sheepishly before starting as if to say 'Don't expect too much. I'm only a jerk'. But when he began he found a part of himself we had never before heard, a deep, crisp, urbane drawl. He appeared to sneer, biting down on the words which almost became the weapon in his hands and Cyrano's coruscating wit came boldly out, spewed out, hissed out.

I watched almost in a state of disbelief at the power and energy and insight coming out of this young actor's mouth. His red hair shaking tremulously over his skull as he snapped back his head to release the fusillade of his wit. Damn good, I thought and I wished I had studied it a bit harder, for it is the play with which we all identify so much. The hero is what all of us actors wish to be. To live like a hero, to be one, to be bold, brave, gutsy, risking life and limb. Risk-taking, madness, cleverness, a stalwart. Yes, all those things which I am and am not, which I want to be, but haven't always the guts, and I'm thinking all those things when I should be concentrating on Terry's piece so I can comment.

Then he finished and was applauded and the group were enchanted, their eyes were shining, the women's eyes were shining for he had revealed another Terry just as Helen had revealed another Helen. It's as if these actors were peeling off layers of skin, psychic layers, and in unpeeling revealing, ardour, passion, power, dynamism. This is in all of us. Yes, and in all of us to reveal it, to bare your soul. To strip naked, naked and raw, your real inner self, not some tart stripping off but a real thunderous raw stripping of all those adipose layers that life wraps us up in like cling film.

"Well done Terry, yes, it was well thought out and moving. I can really see you playing it one day, really ... oh yes, yes absolutely. YES!"

They all made comments since that's what we do, give our thoughts and advice, make suggestions, and now they were waiting for me, they were waiting for me ... my turn, yes, my turn.

MINE.

I have had to make the switch from adviser, leader, to performer, and that's hard, yes, that is very hard. So I suppose I ought to do my bit...

"Go on, go on... we'd love to see your piece ... go on, go, go ... go on."

I moved toward the centre and felt a bit stupid. You're undressed, the eyes are on you, they're looking at the stupid dungarees I'm wearing, my stupid dungarees, the denim ones, and are they not a bit stained, a little shabby since I threw them on thinking how smart I looked. All hippy and arty and now I feel I look like just another tacky, unwashed actor ... the shame.

I began. The words of Macbeth came out slowly and deliberate ... don't race, don't fall into that trap, let them examine you ...let the words just ooze out of your mouth ... deliberate upon the death of your King Duncan, let the words soar for they are soaring, flying images. The words started as they do, or as they should, to take affect like a drug touching all those sensitive parts in the mind's storehouse of memories and I very slowly started to feel the agony of Macbeth, and was now glad I had chosen that speech, for the words fitted his mood. That was my mood. A fearful mood.

I was into it and it was flowing and I could see the others with almost involuntary smiles on their faces, thinking 'Hey ... that's not bad'.

Suddenly, BANG! BANG! A face peeps round the corner ... "Er ... sorry," a mousey voice, everything stops ... "Er ... sorry to interrupt but someone left his motorbike in the courtyard and it's forbidden ... sorry so could you remove it... thank you."

"Oh shit, that's mine ... Sorry I'll be right back!"

And he dashes down the stairs. Cyrano dashes down the stairs having got out his speech with full concentration, full attention and silence, he manages to

FUCK ME UP.

"Go on ... please... it was good."

Their faces saw my disappointment and knew that more was riding on my speech than just approval or testing. It took a lot of guts to go out there in front of those who were speedily becoming my pupils.

"Nah, I'll do it another time."

"Noooo. Noo. We were really enjoying it, it was good. Just start again. Go on."

I step out and actually do begin and it's going well and even better than before. I passed that place in which I was so rudely interrupted before, when I heard out of the back of my brain swift steps, getting louder and approaching. How could he have parked his bike and found another place so swiftly? And the feet getting louder ... 'I hope he's not going to be a cunt and come in at this juncture ... I hope he's smart enough to listen at the door and not fucking burst in like a cunt ... that he is ...'

And so I carried on. And yes, Cyrano the cunt opened the door, but slowly, softly. That was even worse, since everybody's eye suddenly swivelled to the door and then swiftly back to me but the spell was broken. That spell which an actor or a hypnotist can cast. And the cunt Cyrano creaking in, distracting, because the cunt couldn't just fucking wait!

I stopped again, stopped yet again, and sat down. I sat, and I said I'll do it another time when the demons weren't conspiring to trip me up, and they giggled and everything went smooth and they did some exercises, and one of the group was good at mime and so they learned the exercise with a stick in which it changes into all sorts of other things. And it caught everybody's interest since it was a little bit like a magic trick.

And soon after it was over again, until the next week, but it was good and the group were getting to know each other, and sometimes bringing friends in. Soon we must try a play, or even part of one, I said, and they all agreed and nodded with enthusiasm, especially one girl, a woman who was always elated and broadcast her feelings with enthusiasm and was a little barmy, but in the nicest possible way. There was also an older bitch there that was also full of enthusiasm but after in the coffee shop could do nothing but slag off every other actress who was successful in the business. She liked slagging other females off to help her deal with the fact that few ever wanted her, and when they did they seldom wanted her again. It wasn't that she gave such a bad performance, it was all the frou frou that went with it. The drama, her ego, her performance, always her, her and more her. So when she did work and you went backstage she would almost be begging for you to give her love, to spoon it into her greedy mouth and fuck the play and fuck everyone else in the play for it was her, her, and ever more her. Her eyes beamed into yours glittering, expecting the orgasm of approval which she'd store and then at a later time she'd tell you whom she bumped into and how much they said they *loved* my performance!

"They love my work, I know she loves my work" she said. "I inspired her to be an actress, or an actor, and he loves my work, my work, my work, my work!"

But she decided to go to the classes on Saturday. I noticed that she started to flirt with the young male actors. And soon she was sleeping with the actors, and then I suddenly felt a cold, set, slimy chill through my body, as if I felt that she was using me, using the class, not only for company and work but to score nice young men. Oh fuck it. She's a woman. She *has* to look after herself and this is what they do... this is what they do... look after themselves...yes. And don't you do the same? Hmm?

CHAPTER 26

The working man

Hey, this awful fucking useless agent got me an audition for the Globe theatre and so I went and had chat with this bitch who was directing it, and to be directed by a bitch is a hell of a fucking thing to endure, not that I endured it too much, but the few times I'd had to I wasn't very happy since they all seemed to have an agenda. And not my agenda.

However, I got through the experience each time ... just ... but each occasion left a sour taste in my mouth and I was mighty glad to get away from them. Not that I loathed bitches because I didn't, and there were areas in which they could be brilliant like design and sets, but in other areas it was a battle of the sexes. But that puts too simple a gloss on it. It's wanting to be loved, adored.

Joan Littlewood though, was good. She was the best. Absolutely one of the very best. She was a mighty mother!

So I'd gone to meet with the bitch at the Globe and waited and waited and never heard from her again.

Never. Never. Not week after week, just to say thanks but it's not quite right for me and I'll have to choose someone I feel won't intimidate me too much. And she had all her cozzies worked out and like the rank fucking amateur that she was had been round the amateur circuit like the usual Shakespeare Emporiums. And all the set worked out along with the cozzies. But she was an uninterested and uninteresting cow and so I never heard from her again.

And why don't these fucking women ever learn any fucking manners! Cause they don't think they need to. They're women. They're entitled, so they don't believe that they have to, and this has happened nearly every time with women, bitches, whatever. Fuck.

It's not fun to be unemployed.

It's been awhile now. Quite a while. It's as if all the work in the world had dried up and there was nothing left. At least nothing for me. Nothing. And so what to do when you're unemployed? What do you do? Yes, what? Just what? So I go to the YMCA. And that's good cause I get a good work out, sometimes on the weights and sometimes playing handball with the taxi drivers, and so I'd wait until they had finished a game or two and then play the winner, but most of the time they would thrash me after one game and go back to playing their mates again. And so, even here ... yes, even here ... I had to fight for just a little satisfaction. So that one game was usually pretty good and then I'd go into the weights room and work out for a bit. I'd lay on the bench, and two of them, or sometimes one, would stand over me with the barbell and 120, 140, or even 150 pounds on the ends, and slowly lower it onto the protective towel on my chest and then I would

HHHHHEEEEEEEAAAAAAVE

it up and down, and heave it up and down and this would go on for ten sets, and then okay, and then they'd come in quickly and take the weight off my hands and put it back in the stirrups, and then I would do the same for them. And watch them heeeeave it up and down, and up and down, and then if there were two others, the other man would go.

By that time my body had restored it's vital acids, and I would lay on the bench, smelling them, smelling their sweaty bodies, smelling all that male testosterone in the under-washed, under-cleaned gym and the smell was like slightly sour leather, feet, sweat, armpits. And then I might go back and see if there were any second division handball players who I could easily thrash but still have a good sweaty workout, and that was the best feeling in the world. To work out the body and run, and leap and snatch victory, and smash the ball against the wall so my opponent couldn't get it back but would slither and slide and sometimes land on his arse. So handball was the real fave at the gym and there were some first class players there. There were two from the press offices when Covent Garden had the big printing works for Fleet Street and these guys earned a fortune, but always seemed to be in the gym, and their skill was formidable and no matter how hard or how often I played, I could never come even near their breath-taking effortless skill.

Then I'd have a shower and there was much laughing and yakking in the shower where everybody was released after their workout and happy, and would soap each other's backs and be careful not to get too familiar! Then after a good dry put your stinking sweaty gear back in your wire baskets for it to dry, and mould, and stink until you picked it up the next time. That's how it was then. And then upstairs you could just sit in the lounge, that's in the old days. It's different now, now that they let tarts into the YMCA!

So you sit and drink tea and chat and the food was a bit rancid and wanky like the whole place, but there was always something you could get your teeth into. And then you'd chat and chat and chat. And then you'd go home on the 19 bus, still feeling good, still feeling worthwhile, and fresh, and clean, and purged and relaxed, but then you'd go home and there was nothing left … nothing left …

NOTHING.

But there was always the passion, the sex, the occasional trysts which were the source of joy, the essence of life, the fuel which kept heart and soul together, yes, there was always those and there were so many of them, always and ever there. In my book, at the back of my address book, a whole list of them. Just call one and if not her, then another, and so work your way down till one became available. Now the list had shrunk since I was in a 'partnership' and had to plan and be shrewd and cunning and it wasn't always easy when she was home.

So now frustration from my self-enforced 'monkery' leached out of my bones but nature has a way of compensating and lately I had the most luscious, lustful dreams, so beautiful, so lyrical as if some spirit chose to compensate me for my empty nights and my empty arms. Last night she came into my arms and she was beautiful, sensuous, slim, not young, but deeply attractive and her body gave itself to me and she was soft and pale and yearning, and I thrust into her and, yes, it was wonderful, and I touched her and felt her sinuous body and she was yielding and willowy and I felt myself inside her and trying to get deeper inside her and then I woke. I felt calmer, felt better and the dreams were coming more and more frequently.

For sex is like a dream when you are in full and deep wonderful congress with another human being and your life is at the maximum potential since you, in a way, become a god, ready to light fire which will produce life and at that moment you feel like you are in a most wonderful dream ... wonderful, wonderful.

CHAPTER 27

The perfect role

But now the weeds were growing in the small back garden and the cats were shitting in the long grass, and the nights were getting longer, which I loved. Loved this perpetual rhythm of nature and remembered the nice ones, the svelte ones, the sexy gorgeous ones.

When I first started my 'workshops' I went at it with a passion to make them work, and there was a girl who seemed to like me. She was small and very wholesomely pretty, and her name was Sammy, and she came back for a drink since the workshop was now in an old church hall across the road. And how good I felt after the workshops, and enlightened, as if I had achieved something really worthwhile and in that mood she came back and we loved each other with such a wild passion and we were head to toe and feasted on each other's fruits until we sucked them almost dry, and then the wonder of it all, the wonderful sweetness of her. And do you know I have never stopped thinking of that night.

Never really stopped thinking about Sammy and that special night.

NEVER.

But my house was a sanctuary and that's what I always wanted and needed and craved and desired. And it was mine, mine, mine. Oh, how I loved, loved having my own pad. It was wonderful. It could also be a bit lonely, but only sometimes, and you had to cope with that. Sometimes like in the old days when I did short seasons of rep I'd come home to an empty flat (I'd let the top floor). Come home, and it was cold, cold and empty, cold and miserable but then I got the fire going, a gas fire in those days, and the kettle on, and read the mail and then it started to warm up. And then I might try and see if any old tarts were in or available, and if not, at least I was getting back in and warming the house and seeing the cats who they half-looked after upstairs, and then I just might go to the Turkish café up the road which used to exist in the old days and the food wasn't too bad. And then I'd go home and have a hot bath and watch some telly and then go to bed. And when I woke up it was day time and I awoke in my own bed and all was good. So I leapt out of bed immediately and walked up the road to the little Italian café for breakfast and that was really nice. That I liked, and it made me feel really at home since the owner was a loving, typically Italian mother who worked with her son, and he was nice and friendly too, and so she was a kind of surrogate mum for a few minutes each morning when I went there.

Sometimes a friend might meet me there since Islington was full of poor young writers, and this guy was always talking about the same book that he wanted to adapt by Lermontov and had written a screenplay called 'Throb', and apart from that didn't seem to have much to say to me, but he was young and attractive and a bit of a drop out. He would walk past my door and say "Fancy going for breakfast?"

And then we'd go down the road together and it was always good to see a friend when I got back from rep. And then I'd be home and wonder what the fuck I could do with myself when I wanted so desperately to act, and was dying to act, and had so much passion and flux and zip and ideas in my bonce, and I'd try and find stuff to do and be in a strange foul mood.

I'm waiting for the next workshop, but this time we would decide on a play and cast it with the right actors and get it up to speed, and then just find a place to perform it. That would be good, and my mind was startlingly clear and fresh and inspired and searching always for another way. That was before the 'bug'. The 'bug' was a little nasty bastard of an obsession that crawled in one day but that was to be much later.

How did it all happen? Who knows the mystery of these things, but one day I was doing a lovely little Tennessee Williams play at the darling little theatre in Greenwich with my old chum Bruce, who was a jolly good actor, and

Bruce was playing 'Tom' and I was doing the 'gentleman caller' and the director was a pleasant enough fellow whom I almost bullied into letting me read for the role, but when I did read, of course he just had to let me have the part of the 'gentleman caller'. I gave a good audition because it was one of those speeches I had worked on — on and off — for years and I was dead right for the role. It was fun to rehearse with my mate and we were doing really well and getting right under the skin of the part, when there were two lines that got me rattled, and all for no particular reason. Maybe they felt a bit freaky.

I was being a bit smart and it didn't jell and so I went over the lines again and again and again, like I had been injected with a drug and had to keep saying them to test myself that I still knew them and it was driving my poor mind insane! In the middle of a meal, or a walk, or on the train ...

TEST THEM. TEST THEM. TEST THEM.

Like an ugly gremlin was inside me and that was the beginning of those word obsessions ... oh horror, horror, horror! But I got over it and the play was well received, and I got some good reviews and I enjoyed my scene with 'Laura', the poor girl with the limp.

But that was years ago — many years ago.

CHAPTER 28

Peace?

It's gone quiet for a bit since the mad bitch, the one who from time to time siphons off my excess jism, was keeping out of sight which was good for me since she gets waves of madness not unlike most women, it seems, when the mobile never stops. Either she's slurpy lovesick and pretends in her warped fucking mind that I'm in love with the mad cow simply because I'm so horny when I see her, because she's now my only means of sluice control and god I feel a new man once I've deposited my load.

This now causes her to think for me, like 'I know you luv me because of the way you hold me', or 'touch me', or this or that, when it's simply pure unadulterated high grade lust that radiates out and it's lovely for both of us. So why can't it be like we're friends that occasionally open each other's taps? And I never fail to pay something each time on top of a good meal for her and the kid. But then, after her worm-eaten mind begins to interpret every word I said in the blackest most egregious way, and then she's spitting that I've been fucking other women, which would be wonderful since this would certainly prevent me from ever seeing that hag again.

But for an aging lothario she is the perfect goods, at if she wasn't insane, which as I said seems to be the nature of women in this new world society. No, I have sadly no one else, since it takes time for me to gain confidence in my fickle wand that now seems to have a mind of its own. The last time I saw her, which I only did when I felt absolutely compelled, and sat in her ropey, filthy front room, the kid was in his little bedroom and it wouldn't seem right for the child to see his mum go into the bedroom, so since my cock was now ablaze I took it out and gave myself the most delicious hand shandy I've had in years while she cupped my balls and kissed me, and it was simply delicious. After I mopped up I fled into the cold fresh air and felt quite wonderful.

The trouble with this is that each time I see her purely for sexual relief and a bit of a chatter she builds up this fantasy that one day I would leave my partner and ride off with her, a concept that could not be possibly more horrific.

And so this goes on and on and sometimes I do tell her to leave me alone, or leave me in peace but then she starts dribbling her life to me by text, as if this sputum of trivia somehow connects us. So really I would never like to see her again and then feel totally free from the disease of need that poisons my home life, but am getting used to it, and so on it goes.

Had to go to the theatre which I do sometimes when a friend is in it and wants to see a mate come in to have someone to have a meal or drink with after since to go home sometimes to an empty flat is not the nicest thing in the world especially if you're playing a whacking great lead ... oh the horror.

So went to see *Othello* which wasn't bad as far as it goes since the Moor is such a great role which the vile pc wankers have taken out of the canon for actors unless you're black, and so one of the great ball-breakers in history has been taken from me which is a great loss since there is nothing quite like *Othello*.

Even so it was never played that often by a Caucasian, yet it was always there as a temptation, a dragon whose tail you need to pull, or rather, a stallion you have to ride, and so it's now like playing the dramatic piano with a heavy base key missing due to the cuntish directors who never act anyway but make rules, the cunts. When a great white actor takes on the role it scours out his very soul, it sandblasts his viscera with biting verse, the words are swallowed alive like snakes.

'ROAST ME STEEP DOWN DEEP IN GULFS OF LIQUID FIRE'.

It maketh the man and now no more those great passions, no more. Alas but fuck them. Just do the fucking thing yourself one day.

"Yes, by heaven!"

CHAPTER 29

The bitter nag

———

So the years ran on by, and during this time I had made the workshop into something that started to throw out seeds and these seeds became productions and I acted in them and felt triumphant, and my cast were like brothers or the friends I never had, and sometimes I fell out with one or the other, and could never understand how they could turn against me when we were all such a loving and devoted family.

But then, even families take umbrage for some unknown reason.

So what play should we do since we couldn't just do workshops without some goal? And so we decided one day that it should be *Macbeth*. Why? Because I had been teaching part time at a little backwater drama school and had directed the students in a production of *Macbeth*. Since this was the first time I had directed I found the process complete and utter hell. I wanted to do something that was entirely unique and not the usual sloppy simple minded shows I had seen on the London stages for years, and inside my soul I knew there was a way of showing the story that had nothing whatsoever to do with the limited banal staging that had been the norm, that had been accepted as if there was no other way of performing them.

There was a key, or if you like, a symbol that would reveal each scene in a much more dynamic and clearer light. But I didn't what or where the key was so I made them do exercises that sometimes had nothing to do with the play, but the exercises would eventually weave themselves into the story, would nudge something out of the play. The play was primitive, an earthy ancient myth of blood, sex and death.

One day I happened to go to see a young American group that were performing and was astounded, astounded as I had never been before in this life by the sheer vitality and sexiness of it. The opening was the key. It was half human, half animalistic. This was it. And this is what I attempted to do.

And so the time went on, just crawled on, sped on and I got older even if I believed, as we all do, that time will stand still for a while and soon, yes soon you'll find the escape you need … that you really do need so badly.

But now with her and the kid it's impossible to leave. It's just impossible for they not only depend on you, but will crumble like clay, just crumble into dust, since you are the molecules that hold the world together for them. Even if you sniff around the corners of the city, sniff around in the dusty, dirty holes, where you might get a sniff of minge, a bit of a thrill, this is the way you've been going on.

In this way I was able to come home, to, smile, to be relieved and even happy until the nag, the bitter nag in the groin came again, and you lay there and you were in torment as you lay there next to a body that you couldn't begin to touch, couldn't begin to go near, and so you both lay there under the thundering darkness and waited for sleep, waited to be carried to the other domain where the sirens and the nymphs touch and caress you in sweet dreams. And the sleep would come since you drank, you drank, you drank, and ate and grew fat and watched the telly. You watched and watched and watched the telly and sometimes friends came, but my mood was on minge.

But when the minge goddess got pissed off with the infrequent visits and threatened to piss off, as she did from time to time, I did feel a sense of relief for now I could be myself again and be rid of the siren beckoning me with promises of squeezing my ample cock.

Now it's been six weeks since I felt her lovely wet minge slide down my shaft and I was feeling that now was the time, when she said, 'No! Fuck off and no more minge, no more sweet pussy until you make me the centre of your life', and this is what they all do. Narrow the goal posts a few inches each time and each time they are peaceful only for a while and then they want you to take them out, to introduce them to your friends which of course you cannot do. And then they, or she, want to be taken to the theatre or to a movie or to an event which you also cannot do without the dangerous possibility of colliding with those who know your life, and so you hold onto the goal posts like Samson.

And then when she or they know, get the feeling that you absolutely need their cunt as if it's the last thing on earth, then they play with you and torment you. But now I said leave me alone when she said she couldn't see me until I got rid of my wife. They all say this after a while. But this wasn't the deal at the beginning, since she knew from the beginning that I had a wife and child and was never, ever, going to leave them. Some men do. They do again and again, and I don't know how they do that. I just don't know how they could leave two members of their family in such pain. I have never known how they can be so cold and callous and how they can, but they do. Yes, they do! And then, surprise, surprise, they do it again! I'm not callous or cold like that.

So one day when I was out and therefore was already on some trivial business, and didn't have to lie when I left the house which I found difficult, I had an excuse. I rang, rang and said I was free. And at first she said, nice, come round, but then she left another message saying, no don't come round, don't. You can't come round just for sex and go off again and leave, leave her wallowing in a loneliness, which is all the more felt, all the more suffered after an hour of squelching shimmering fucking, while you just go home to a nice cosy house and sit with your nice cosy woman, just sit and eat and talk and drink and watch TV. All squelched out and comforted. All purged and siphoned out of the rage, the fire, the sulphur and lava, all squirted, squelched out. But now no.

NO!

And so I was lame and pointless, aimless and limp, unformed since I was formed when I was a man inside her mouth or cunt and pumping away, then I was, yes then I was a man. Then I felt like a man, because what else makes you feel like a man, since there is little else like it that makes you feel every centimetre of your being.

Fuck it and find someone else. Fuck it, but the numbers had dried up. The phone numbers had fallen into disuse, had faded, changed. So, grumpy, deadly, empty, bereft, I decided to try yet again a massage parlour, something I hadn't used for a long time, not since the last sexless relationship with the last woman.

And there was a seedy looking parlour, a dreadful filthy looking place in Shoreditch which I had passed many times and looked at the drab, dirty facade and thought that this might spell something tasty within. Maybe, it's worth a try, shall I? And so since the cab was at the lights I said, 'This is ok and I'll get out here'. And so I paid and got a receipt for the accountant, and thought, don't linger, just do it quickly, go down the dark dirty steps and ring the bell.

After a while a plumpish tart came to the door, but I didn't look like someone who needed relief since I was still a reasonably attractive middle aged man, and she said "We don't really massage here, we have other things."

And I said "Yes, I know and that's what I want."

"I mean other things", she added, like she was some kind of demented dolt, which of course she was.

And I began to think, oh does she mean, whips and chains and such like. And I said, "Well I want extras. Yes, I do like hand relief."

Such a British term, sounding like a nurse was aiding you in your death throes. So when she understood once and for all that it was alright she led me downstairs to a sleazy stale room, off of which were some cubicles. But before this she mentioned that hand relief was an extra fifty quid which I thought a bit high on top of the massage, so I got into the room and removed my jeans but kept my underwear on, and socks.

Then she came in, in a whitish uniform, looking fat and sluttish but not unfriendly and then I removed my knickers and top but kept my nice white woolly socks on and turned over as instructed.

She applied a little oil on my back end started rubbing away, up and down and then getting to the bum, which made it a little more pleasant and then she asked if I wanted it 'topless' which I couldn't care less about. She said that was an extra ten. But you said fifty all in? Yes, but that's just the hand relief which didn't really make any sense. So I thought, fuck it, she's a loathsome fat thief so for an extra ten let it go but the hard-on that was developing went right down after that … so she carried on and got to my arse again and gently touched my balls and it was feeling real nice as her hand slid up the inside of my thigh, and my thick was getting big, and she turned me around and went to work again. Starting at the top, and working down until she had my cock in her hands and it felt really good.

This went on for a bit and there was a mirror opposite to where she was squeezing my cock and so she kept staring into it. By this time she had taken off her white uniform and was standing in a pair of large black knickers, her fat arse bulging out of them and her plump little tits standing out which I perfunctorily stroked as I felt just a twinge, a small twinge, of lust. Eventually and with a little effort I poured the little devil out of my cock and was so glad to have got rid of it, and felt instantly relieved.

The fat slug stopped almost immediately, tore off a shred of the very paper I had been laying on to mop myself up and left the room. There were no towels, nothing to wipe the spunk or grease off with so I took one of the paper sheets out of a box and wiped myself down. I could not even see a basket. Just drop the filth on the floor. The poor devils were crushed in paper where once they were nicely shot into a hot, sticky, warm, wet vulva.

Then I dressed, paid her the money and swiftly leapt up the steps with abandon and relief to be out of that filthy squalid hell-hole. Even the polluted air of Shoreditch felt cool and clean after that pissoir, that charnel house.

CHAPTER 30

Desperate release

I walked up the Bethnal Green Road and noticed everything now I didn't have her knickers on my mind. Now I had got rid of that image, the window in my mind was clear and there was a world out there. I guess I was, or even am, an addict. Never used to be but something has crawled into my mind. Some surreptitious devil has hoodwinked its way into my unconscious found some nourishing pasture there and bedded down for the duration. I tried, for years I've tried, but I can't beat this addicition.

Now the bastard bug has been spat out and the devil will have to spend some time getting his ammunition together and for a few weeks I will have a breather. And yes, the fresh air ... aaaaah.

I crossed the road and entered the famous and notorious Brick Lane and entered the all-night bagel house. What it is about that filthy grimy Brick Lane that is attracting all the little nobodies from the safe and wholesome parts of England? The place always had a grubby feel about it and the women on shift that morning were a shifty, scurrilous bunch. The salt beef for the sandwiches sat in the window and for hygiene, and I use the word loosely, they had draped a bit of wrapping paper over it. I ordered 6 bagels with two already stuffed with smoked salmon and cream cheese since I knew my missus had the odd craving for one, her family being Czech and all that. An old gremlin served the bagels in her slovenly, slothful way and I grabbed my plastic bag and ambled down the road and waited for a black cab.

Now as has often happened in the past, her cutting off all relations, which was a relief in more ways than one, also seemed to trigger in her a sheer vomitorium of anguished whiney chords. This would go on for some time. Lengthy moans of how I won't stay the night, or go on trips without her and all this would go on filling my mind with the noisome activity of a star about to implode. The foul spew went on until the early hours and then carried on the next day. It might stop for a few hours and then lo and behold the stinking little volcano would erupt again.

However, it was a time when a small job called me out of the home and this presented an opportunity for naughtiness which of course I now did not have. The curse hit the fan some days ago when I sneaked out on the pretence of visiting my mother in Cliftonville and hoping to perhaps have an opportunity to sniff around for spare minge, when at the same time the beast called and sloshily recalled the time when we would go to the coast together. Excitedly I called back to say the opportunity had now by chance arrived, and I would take her to the coast where we could fuck and suck our little hearts out.

However — oh the irony — she now said that she no longer wanted to and blamed me for not taking her years ago, and the whine to which she was so sorely addicted began once again in earnest. By nightfall she was texting like a lunatic while I chose to ignore her rants. Nevertheless, she did the one unforgivable thing that all whores, mistresses, tarts and part-time girlfriends know ... *Never do you ring your lover at their house. Never. Never. Never!* This is not in the deal. Not in the contract, since what we, the mistress and I, have is precious, secret, tasty, lascivious and don't shit on it! But

MAD BITCHES DO!

The first call I caught in my other room and hastily whispered ... "Don't call here. Use the mobe."

But just as I am sitting down to supper the mad beast calls the main line again and this time my permanent mad bitch picks it up and the lunatic is of course on the line asking for me. My clever bitch gives her good short shrift and cuts her off with a choice and pithy snub. But lo and behold, the scumbag calls my wife on her mobile, and when my missus picks it up, hears my voice speaking. You see the raddled and mentally diseased scumbag had kept all my loving messages and played them back to my astonished and then very distressed old lady! What a vile thing to do. So I swiftly texted her back saying that the police have been called. Then the calls stopped. That's the end of that. I may for some reason have used my wife's mobile and she must have kept the number. Stupid of me!

Quiet for a while, then the next day, having purged herself the slime bag starts sending whiny texts … 'Sorry for having given you a bad time but I've been ill and overworked blah blah. And although you're wicked, I don't want you out of my life…', and this pleased me somewhat for I was just contemplating where I could get some old friendly minge that had long gone off the boil, and trying to remember old numbers.

But the mad bitch and me were still sexually squelchy for each other's genitalia and so the bitch still had a hold. So I did a small audition and not too well for my head was full of squirm, and then I called and said I'll come over for bit, and she whines.

"I'm not well and have a cold and the cat has given me sore eyes and I've got the curse."

But I said "Doesn't matter."

And she whined "Oh well alright then."

And then I leapt into a cab to the slag's flat. I even bought some cake and some fruit for the ill patient… I rang the bell but she didn't let me in for a while but eventually I heard her pounding down the stairs which has me thinking that she wants to go for a coffee and I won't be allowed to get my cock out, but it transpires that the entrance bell wasn't working.

She looked like death, white as a ghost and I tip-toed up the stairs after her to her grimy room which never ever looked as if it got cleaned and although she knows I'm coming makes no attempt to clean up. My cock is out and I want her to squeeze and suck if she can't fuck cause of the curse, which I seem to have weirdly timed my visits to coincide with, but she wants to make some tea and put it away. She says she'll play with it later.

So I do, and in the meantime listen to her stream of consciousness which is like a stream of undiluted junk from a city's sewers, toilets, wastelands, factories; industrial effluent all spewing out since now she has a pair of ears in which to pour it all out, and on and on she rants about this one and that one who has let her down, or betrayed her, or not paid her for some job, and on and on.

And I hmmn and ahhh and occasionally nod and the sofa is full of bits of junk, old mobiles, letters, diaries, dead watches, old grubby clothes. This sofa on which I have been fucked by her so many times since she bestrides me and fucks the life out of me, which she does really well and sometimes crouches since she has a strong pair of legs...

Ok, so let me wank and hold my balls.

"But what's in it for me?" she whines.

Well let's fuck, doesn't matter about the curse for now my whole raison d'etre is to pump, and she says not on the sofa since it may leave a mess, we'll do it in the bedroom on a towel. So we go into the even more scrubby, dishevelled, dirty, bedroom where she lays the towel on the bed and goes into the bathroom to pop out her rag and then comes back. I've been squeezing my cock to get it ready and she bestrides me and licks her finger and then used it to lubricate her cunt since there is never any foreplay. And then, yes, then I feel the slick, slow slide down over my shaft and it's

DELICIOUS, FANTASTIC, WONDERFUL, HEAVENLY, AT LAST, THE REAL THING.

And on she pumps, bouncing, slips, pulls, wriggling her arse for more traction. She's leaning backwards which makes her cunt grip all the harder onto my cock and oh it's delicious, really juicily delicious, and I lay back on the bed arching my crutch into her and then she slides off, just for a bit, and asks me to get on top which now I love to do all the more for having been spoilt, and I sink my cock into her and it's hard enough to slide in, but once it's in it seems secure, and I slide and slither, push and pull, and this time my mouth is on hers and so I feed on her mouth and tongue, feed on them while my cock is drilling below and my mouth above and pumping and moaning, and now I begin to feel the spunk ready to shoot out, feel that ecstatic moment when you are on the point of no return and you just have to let it out and you don't even have to move anymore, don't have to pump and slither, just feel the cock arching and ready to do it's number, and you just remain still to feel it, to let it open itself out and let your brains fly out with it.

OUT, SPURT, SPURT!

Then, slowly, a few more strokes but then it's out, out, get out, slither out, pull out and relief, its out, lay a respectful time on the bed but not too long. She is not a lover that you can endure those moments after sex with. You're on the floor, you're in the bathroom and wash your cock carefully with soap and water and towel off and now you're better, yes, much better. And you sit and finish the tea which was made half hour ago. She washes and comes back in with fresh knickers on, and tights, and so the miraculous part of nature is for the moment finished. Completed, when for a few moments you reflected the original universal big bang. When you scattered your sperm like galaxies, like the Milky Way, and new worlds were created.

And now you're calm it's time just to raise a couple of issues which you weren't able to raise pre-orgasm. Weren't able to raise less the psycho locked up the shop when you were really

DESPERATE.

But now in a calm way you might just air your grievances as to why she thought it necessary to ring your *fucking home*. Why it was necessary to ring my wife's mobile and leave one of my old sex messages and what an infamous act, what a treacherous act, what a vile thing to do. And so I said

WHY?

And she said in the nature of great psychotic liars that she wasn't aware. That she didn't know. And I said (lying), the police were informed but I stopped it going further, and with that she went into one of her serpent's spitting rages of how I got sex out of her and then threaten her with the police for leaving lovely sexy messages. But she got the police on me for leaving *porn* on her phone and for making obscene messages, and so, pulling my sweater she said,

"Go on, get OUT!"

So with great relief I sped down the stairs while she shouted after me,

"And take the fruit, take the bananas you bought, I couldn't bear to eat them now."

"Shove them up your arse... " I spat back as I so gratefully escaped into the cool refreshing street.

Oh, now it's over I thought and dearly hoped. Oh thank god. But as I walked down the street, as is my nature, I began to worry. Just a little tiny cell of fear. And doubt began to creep into my brain. Would she perhaps go to the police again and make up the story that I was sending her obscene calls as she did before, when she was feeling smug at the time, and probably had some new cock and was feeling powerful.

But the thing is like a disease that keeps returning and I, in my weakness after a few weeks, do return to the filthy scene of the crime even when I swear to myself that this is, this has to be, the last time. The last time!

So I rang the cow and spoke and she had settled a bit, and 'Let's part as friends', I said. And 'Yes', she said, all calm. So I thought, no, she wouldn't go to the cops again like a filthy lying blackmailer, and I went back to work.

CHAPTER 31

Out, damned spot!

MACBETH My dearest love, Duncan comes here tonight.
LADY MACBETH And when goes hence?
MACBETH Tomorrow, as he purposes.
LADY MACBETH O, never shall sun that morrow see! Your face, my thane, is as a book where men may read strange matters......

The group met at the little church hall across the road, which I had been smart enough to rent at a reasonable rate from a very nice vicar, and as soon as I entered the room I felt clean, clear, and as I trod those nice sanded floor boards my soul was at peace. Yes, I felt at long last at peace, and I sucked in the air. It was my, *my* workshop and it was my church, if you like. Yes, this was *my* church and I felt I was the servant of the church, a kind of high priest, and here we only devote ourselves to what is worthy.

The actors dribbled in and hung up their coats and put their shoulder bags or rucksacks down and one sod came on his bike and it was a whole business seeing him get out of his bike clothes and take off his bike shoes, and bring in his wet-wheeled bike which left its spore mark across the floor and then he got into his woolly, flared dance pants which we all wore in those olden days. And then he rarely stopped suggesting things, none of which I cared for, until at last I used to dread him coming down the road on his bike since he came with so much baggage. But underneath he was a decent enough chap.

And then Pip came in who I really loved, since he gave so much and suggested always the most fascinating ideas as he had studied a whole world of movement. He had a cheekiness and inventiveness in his whole being. His entire body was alive to life, so brilliant, so pragmatic in that smart, savvy northern way, and a big bushy head of hair, and I was happy just to clap my eyes on him.

He had a good take on the witches, a very good one. By bending forward and pulling his arms back behind and up, he resembled a vulture and he entered the spirit of the act with such abandon that he made you see the beast.

Pip brought in a couple of his mates since we needed some more people, and since they came by his suggestion they were always interesting performers. Glyn was sleek with long jet black hair and a superb mover. Then there was my ex-lover from Glasgow and she was not only beautiful but had a certain style and entered into the spirit as we all did for we felt that we were special and had a goal and were united as an ensemble. We were proud, we were focused, and we were alive and alert. Not to the schmoozy, seedy world of the actor as piss artist and imbiber in late night clubs, who had not the slightest feeling for movement, or sound, or love of their own art. They were loud and brash and somewhat ghastly.

We were another world. A new world in which the hall was our church and here we worshipped and this we did five times a week. Even when I stupidly broke my ankle being too ambitious in the gym and was confined to a wheelchair we carried on.

I took my assistant Chris from a drama school that was just about surviving in the more mildewed areas of Kensington. Chris was an American and had a natural easy swagger and was very smart and of course I loved him, as I loved all of them. They were there for me, as they knew I was there for them.

In the early evening I crossed the road to the church hall and unlocked the door. As I crossed the road I saw the kids playing in the street with no real purpose, just an idle flopping around from post to post, an idle doodling with their lives, their games formed from nothing and I thought what a damn shame that they don't have and will never have such manifest joy as I will have. Even through pain when I dithered and knew not what to do and we went over and over the same bit because it had become an obsession in my head, and I was searching for the perfect way, the right way, the most inventive way of imparting information, I still felt I was on the true path.

Oh how nervous was I the time I organised the first rehearsal ... oh how fearful. But of course what you fear the most you just have to do and the fear slowly, gradually turns alchemically into strength.

So we start with a warm up, a series of exercises designed, so we thought, to open us up, make us relaxed, stimulate our imaginations, release our inhibitions, make us flexible, give us new skills, make us wiser, more inventive. The alternative is the wanker directors who just sit and talk, sit and talk, talk and sit, until the actors go mad from frustration. That's *their* way, and what a dull, negative frustrating way it is, and somehow full of fear for not facing the subject straight on. At least I never talked about the subject. I was too shy and in some ways did not want to seem like a guru spouting bollocks when it was the actors we wish to see, so just start.

But we did all these bloody warm ups so in my own way I was a bit evasive, but knew in my heart that these exercises were often used, or filtered their way into the work. Some of the exercises were taken from the mime classes I once attended so assiduously when I was a young actor, and had never forgotten them and had embellished and used them as a basis to create new ideas, and I was thankfully never short of ideas.

And so we did our hour of exercises and impros, and Pip led the way with his startling inventions. Sometimes we just did exercise and work on the mat. One of which was to put three or four chairs on the floor laid in a row and leap over them into a forward roll, somersaulting over them and then adding one at a time until we had six. But only Pip would leap over the six! He was a daring bugger.

Women came and went as is their want, but some stayed the course. But now we were getting really inventive and after each rehearsal we would go to the local pub and have a well-earned pint and we were all so excited and fulfilled and each night when we left I saw the same dreary dispossessed kids playing aimlessly in the street, and I thought we had touched bliss. Especially if it had gone well.

Once there was a charming girl called Blanche, who had recently come in to replace the endless parade of witches who came, and I asked her back for a drink since I was only across the road and we soon crawled into bed. And being a director and seemingly in charge of events makes you quite desirable to young women I guess, but at the time I was not to know this.

And so this went on for months until the time came to find a theatre in which we could show our work. We had created a work on our own. A unique work. A different work. A special work. A work which was covered in our finger prints and owed nothing to the tossers who were running our theatres, those wanked out hacks who paraded the same mindless unimaginative crap over and over again. Night after night we all met, and that church hall was our life, our salvation, our manna from heaven. This is where we made communion with the bard, with language, with god, and it felt good.

And lo and behold, the time came and we just went

on and did it. We gave it our all. On the first run in the theatre I was exhausted after the first five minutes since we had created a symbolic battle scene, but after that initial shock I took it more easily.

We invited the critics after the first few previews and were full of optimism having accepted the audience's enthusiasm as a guide to its success. The first reviews were due out on the Sunday and so after the Saturday night performance I dashed out to get the Sundays that were already on sale at midnight. Hastily I thumbed open the papers and read the reviews. Dreadful! I couldn't believe the scathing, cynical tripe I was reading. It was not just a bad review. It was a dumb bum review from a stale old fart in a dull grey Sunday paper. Too old, too tired and set in his abominable ways to even begin to understand where we were going with Shakespeare.

SOD THE BITCHES!

Such a shame, for it depleted our audiences at first, but they still came. It made us all even more determined. Perhaps there were some crude moments in the production that l had not yet the skill to be aware of, but so much of it was so unlike any of the sheer unadulterated rubbish I had been seeing for years apart from the rare exception which was Brook's *Lear*, or Dexter's *Othello*. The rest you could bury.

The bitches buried us well and truly, but we kept going with great enthusiasm. But then we came to the end of the road. A good team of actors but it was to be the last time I worked with most of them except my dear devoted and adorable Pip. I enjoyed being Macbeth even if a slightly bizarre one. Having no costume designer we just wore silly black dyed string vests and black tights and bare feet. Some thought it was like a dance.

Glyn was a good 'Banquo' and a fantastic 'Porter' and the best one I had ever seen. Through a mimed door came the actors as the characters he described and they were hysterical. The dagger was transported by a circle of sleeping arms who were the dinner guests at the first meeting and who then settled down to sleep. Now as I write these lines all these years later, there is a germ in me that wants to do it again and now it would be better than ever.

Some ideas I pinched since we were all pinching ideas then, and we pinched some stuff from a group who no doubt pinched their stuff, and so on, and so forth. But we persevered and at least we did put it on and expressed the play which was more than the poor dumb, stale, flaccid critic could do, and we touched a little bit of heaven and that made us happy and no one can be happier than an actor playing a long difficult role and getting through it. But that was then. And that gave us a foundation to keep going even though it became more and more difficult the more we challenged ourselves to be even better next time. So thank you wherever you all are, all the others, who were so good and giving, thank you all, all, all, all, all, all.

CHAPTER 32

This madness

It was about that time when I met my future wife. That was way before the witches. Way before the scumbags. Way before the emotional blackmailing hags. It was a good time.

So our production of *Macbeth* was not only a super hit in my mind but also it showed me what can happen when you start with a few collywobbles in your gut, what you can achieve out of your fear, and the bigger the fear, sometimes, the larger the reward. It showed that we could do it and those muscles in the head from all those months of turning up in our little church hall gave me the power, gave me the key to opening the door to doing this again. Do it again and be bolder than ever. Challenge the impossible. That's what you have to do.

Of course the addiction had to start again. It's like a bad habit, like smoking that you can't do without, no matter the health risks. And it builds up after a while and you feel you need a puff even if you think you will never need to smoke again after stubbing another filthy butt out in the ashtray. Yes, it had to start again, but it's fading out thank god, just like my lust is thankfully fading out.

But when my wife and kid had to go away for a few days to see her family it gave me an opportunity to be totally free and not scuttle home like a furtive guilty rat. Just free in heart and spirit.

I found it difficult to rehearse with that thing in my mind and I found my wife's last few days difficult to deal with since I had that dirty image in front of my nose and I just couldn't wait for her to go. Please go. I couldn't even, speak properly. Couldn't find the freedom inside myself to be me.

WHO AM I?

And so I waited for her to go and the nights were the worst after she made dinner and I tried to tell her how the day was, and make it interesting, and then I'd plonk myself in front of the box like a heap of dung. Just plonk my fat arse in front of that ghastly mind sucking box, that filthy human stew. Just sat there and waited to get pissed after quaffing a bottle of wine and then some more until I could feel tired and plonk into bed, and what a life. Oh, what a life ...

Got to get rid of the horrible siren bitch who has me by the cock but then I am drawn almost by an act of possession. After I never ever want to see the thing again since she keeps sending little messages as if she thinks this keeps me on the back burner, and I really want to get rid of her forever.

PLEASE. PLEASE. PLEASE!

However, after the missus had gone, the very day she left, I called. Left a message, usually the one word variety ... like "supper?" And waited. But nothing came through since when I do actually leave a message she knows that the horn is leading me to the drug, and she can play the game.

But eventually she said "Let's do supper."

And so we went to a really nice place but she had her kid with her which I didn't expect but didn't mind since he has to live too and we went and had a really good meal which I enjoyed since I seem only to really enjoy my life these days when I am sitting amongst the throng in a nice cosy café.

So we sat and they ordered everything they would not normally be able to afford. But now the cock is buying so make hay while the cock is hungry and so we all ate and drank and went back to her slum up the road. But now we have to wait to hit the bed since the little bugger is wide awake. It's not late after all and he wants to watch TV. So I had to sit there and watch the biggest pile of shit I ever thought I would be forced to watch. It was some kind of parlour game with England's greatest wanking tosspot sitting in the centre as the game host, while the other tossers answer idiotic questions and try to be witty. I could barely hold onto my mind which was slowly being boiled alive, but then it was over and then he was ordered into bed and then I got my cock out and then she sat on it, sucked it, wanked it and then I sunk it into her and came... oh thank god. Then I escaped back to my lovely clean, pure home.

Lovely. Lovely. Yes, to be home, but now I was alone and the kind of friends I have, the kind of tossers I have been seeing for years, can't even reply to my calls when I suggest a dinner and a chat, time to get together. So I left messages but no one answered, like I had leprosy. And one guy I rang who was quite successful and with whom I have never ever had a meal without his missus there, said he was busy and had to check a show, which was ok, but I never heard back from him again. The other ponce did ring back to apologise for not ringing back, but then I found my old ally was free. My old acting ally who was dependable as the wind and the rain, and we met up to see a poxy little play that had received glowing reviews and of course I always note the critics who give glowing reviews to shit while castigating my work, and I realise that they are impotent, artistically

IMPOTENT.

They have joyless brains. They are artless. Can only see what is real and in front of them and can never understand the gesture, the idea, the game, the symbol, the language of the theatre, but only the language of the text and even then not too well.

I was working again, and at last, and got the guys together and it was good to see them again. We all chatted and told each other what had been going on since Macbeth and how we all missed working and doing our stuff, and how exciting it was, and no matter what the cunting critics said the audiences were overwhelmed and that was the main thing, not the daft worn out prats who get a weekly wage to sit through pretentious plays, and is it any wonder that they become somewhat jaded.

But to finish, to try to get to the end of this farrago, this madness. There was only one more time and that was that, when the need gets to you and the need turns into a compulsion, and the compulsion to an obsession. And so it was on one of those days, when up to then I had thought I'd got rid of the beast. Over I traipse but now it's day time and the kid is still there, which of course she fails to mention, so the poor kid always feels like his life is in the way.

We go to a pleasant little Arabic bistro for a snack and I'm just dying to fuck it, to have my fix. But the kid's there, she says, but if I actually pay the kid to go out and buy a sweater that he's had his eye on, if I give him £50, for that then he'll go out and buy it for himself, and be very glad to do so since he's had his eye on that particular sports sweater for weeks.

So we went back and I peeled off some notes and he smiled and was happy and she removed her tampax (my timing has been very poor lately). With certain men when the need comes they could fuck even a plague victim. There is nothing certain men will not fuck when that particular need is upon them, and so I emptied my jism into her with a great big sigh.

THAT'S ALL.

So I did, and it flooded out of me and that's not a bad feeling. In fact it's a wonderful feeling for an oldie. It is wonderful but among the female race there are a few bizarre bitches that see this as a source of power over you and wish to enforce this even when I have repeatedly stated that I am with another woman, and have been for over twenty years, and this is a strong relationship.

But of course it is patently obvious that the carnal side of things has little to do with love at this stage and demands fulfilling no matter what the state of feeling is between the protagonists.

So I start to feel trapped when she persists in sending me messages as if to claim her right over me. Even when I don't reply still they come, wishing me well, and hope the show is going well, and I hope you are healthy and not too tired, and all manner of meaningless simpering little darts to try and nail me down and keep me in a false sense that we are a happy swinging couple. And it's like acid being spat on me, each message with its gluey, syrupy shlosh is like cat vomit, and I ignore it and tell her not to keep sending messages since it disturbs me when I want to work.

But she keeps on and when I'm at home I can't feel that glorious sense of abandonment, that glorious sense of being alive, alive and free. So I decide to write calmly since I know she's a bit of a lunatic and is prone to insane tantrums and behaviours (like leaving a message on my landline), and so I calmly texted that it would be better if we remained friends since I can't lead a double life anymore and it's too disturbing.

And I sent this and felt immediately better, and lighter, and freer, but within a short while after anxiously staring at my mobile from time to time, a message came through saying that I am obviously having a bad day and then went into the usual meaningless drivel and chatter.

And so I texted back that I meant it and that it would be better to remain just friends as *she had herself suggested* some time ago. And the better feeling returned again, the cleaner feeling, surer feeling, the feeling of lightness, since I don't want to be tempted again like Ulysses tied to a mast and hearing the sirens singing their filthy songs – and one can only imagine what they sang. Songs of the rarest purest filth imaginable, songs that knew the hearers' weaknesses and deepest unfulfilled desires, songs of unimaginable pleasures. Only by tying himself to the mast could he possibly escape from the torment. And in such a way must I too ignore the slithery siren bitchy snake for the cost is now too high, far too high, and let me be free ... yes, free for a while if not forever, please!

Now she's sending messages again about how I am living with a prison warder who only lets me out from time to time. She is not, so she doesn't wish to wait endless weeks for when I am let out!

So show me a man who is not living with a warder and vice versa. It's a shame but that's the price you pay if you want a mate, friendship, loyalty, a meal on the table, your smalls washed, a companion to go out with, take trips with, entertain your friends, be an ally, stand by you, listen to your problems and your pains, check your work, give you hope, make you feel better, tolerate your lousy relatives and support them too in difficult times, but if you want that dreamy, creamy sex and flashing knickers you have to be sneaky and subtle, and be careful not to hurt, unless you're an animal. A beast that doesn't give a damn. A low type of muff chaser that will sacrifice all for a night of fucking, irresistible as that may be, and doesn't care about the poor bitch at home.

Once a bitch senses that you're hooked on snatch like a poor thrashing dangling fish, once she senses that you're well and truly hooked, you slowly but surely become her dog, her pet, her servant, her treasure chest to do with you what she will, and for some reason best known to the female gender it also seems to inspire some sadism. To play with you. To tease you, abuse you, insult you and even accuse you of all sorts of wretched crimes. Just cause they know that their cunt has shot off the Richter Scale. Once the shares in cunt have gone through the roof, this naturally gives them a sense of power over the male. And the bitch finds this power intoxicating and it's like a drug that sends them flying.

So you have to hang onto the remnants of your poor soul as long as you can or you will be well and truly 'fucked'.

The last time this happened, the last time I was reduced to a slobbering canine so grateful for the odd pat was with a bitch who had me leaping through hoops and even sinking into the deepest darkest pit where you will tolerate almost anything just to be permitted the occasional plunge into minge. She had found a new lover who was more available than yours truly, although by this time I was indeed making myself more available when I saw she was slipping away, and causing the consequent chaos and distaste in my own home.

But having found her new lover it seems that he was also of restricted availability during the week and only available at the weekends and so I was permitted to call or even visit during the weekdays as long as I kept well away during their long weekends together. No matter, for some time I put up with it and in many ways it suited me as well, but as the weekends rolled around I felt slightly sick to the stomach at the idea of my precious one being stuffed by another's fat scummy cock and so the weekends passed by in wretched torment.

And when I resisted the temptation to call on her 'days off' she would say things like "Now you're getting better, you're learning…"

Needless to say, one day she pissed off for good and I lost a lot of weight, which goes to show that every cloud has a silver lining.

Several months later she started to call me again, since obviously things weren't working out too well with her scummy lover but by then it was too late, I had found a new 'bitch.'

CHAPTER 33

Summer loving

Summer is here at last, and of course it sends its heat into the deepest, darkest recesses of the body and each woman you look at seems a potential feast and so in this mood I actually called the beast. But she said oh, how nice but she was going to see her kid at his public school and wouldn't be back till 4pm, and so I texted back that 4pm would be fine and had dizzying fantasies of squelching together on the couch.

Then she texted back that she would be hungry and could we go to some fancy restaurant since that would be near the station. I had a suspicion that she was conning me yet again and that this was an opportunity to screw an expensive dinner out of me for her and her kid. Normally I wouldn't mind since I have taken them both out dozens of times but I felt that this was an opportunity for her to drag him along without telling me. Like springing the poor fucker on me and nix to a shag after since the kid was around.

But she never once said that she had the kid with her, and would I mind, but in her cunning conniving and thieving way, she just springs him on me. She's like a low grade thief, and not even a smart thief. So I watched from across the road and saw the two of them marching into this beautiful expensive café like a couple of low gypsy thieves and I felt sick of both of them. However I took a deep breath and went across the road and met the pair with my long face and resolved never to take her there again ... ever. Of course she encourages her son to choose the most expensive dish on the menu and he was the only kid in the place since children don't go there. She stuffed herself too while I had only a soup since I had eaten already. I was so glad to get out and flee. I said I had to go, and so couldn't take her home on top of everything.

Anyway, I said I had no cash left and have to get to a cash point where quick as a feral cat she said "We'll walk with you." She was expecting a bit of a hand out, after having conned me for a slap up meal but I withdrew my dosh and said goodbye and pissed off. That's the last time I'm seeing the filthy beast. The last time!

For a while there were some abusive messages as there always is but I let it go. And then an old colleague texted to tell me that he had been receiving messages from the beast! How she complained to him who she hardly knew, and writing the most private things about me. That's when I thought that, that was truly it. That I would be insane to even consider seeing the lunatic again since it seems to increase the poison within her to discharge at a later date.

It would be folly even to try to describe the volley of texts I received after I confronted her with the info I received from my friend. Apparently she had emailed him with a series of complaints about me including some of the most foul, where I had, in trust, confided elements of my life pertaining to my poor late departed sister whom I had gone to see shortly before she died, and the callous and despicable slug wrote that I was so heartless that I didn't even go to see my dying sister.

My nice and elegant friend wanted to warn me, since the filthy venomous slag had been writing a noxious column as scum does these days on the foul internet. On confronting her she was so amazed she practically exploded into filthy little pieces like Rumplestiltskin and swore that she had never ever sent my friend messages, or maybe once when she was in a peeve about me, but this was beyond the pale. Her messages came through fast and furious and I was only worried that she might burst and spill her ordure on the phone of my missus, which was one of her tricks, but soon it abated when I just begged her not to use my phone as a dustbin for her ravings, and for some reason this shut her up for a while.

And then, lo and behold she got rid of all the filth she had written on her Facebook page, which did not use my name even, and if it was, according to my friend, based on me. And this was while I was seeing her and taking her out with her son for nice meals, and having the occasional terrific bunk up in her filthy bedroom, which is about the grimiest bedroom I had ever seen in my life and never looked as if it had ever been clean. Never mind it was

OVER

and there was peace in my heart, and no longer fear of the phone ringing at all hours or my mate's phone filled with her stringy phlegm-filled poison.

Things got a mite desperate, the result of which induced a desire in me just to have a woman's hands on my body so I whisked into Soho where I noticed a Thai massage centre which to all purposes looked just like a straight good massage and so for 50 quid I treated myself. My masseuse had the face of an angel which made me feel all the more like an ungainly aging lump of overblown flesh. Her hands moved swiftly and deftly and worked their powerful little fingers into the spongy lava that covered my muscles, carefully avoiding too close a proximity to my 'lunatic parts'.

Eventually it came to an end. Yet she hovered, and said she could do another half hour. By this time my cock was just aching for a little 'comforting' if not even shedding a little tear. So seizing the moment I dipped one hand under the towel and grabbed my lonely little sausage to which, and to my amazement, she confessed that if I paid her £20 more she could 'do it' or I wank while she just massaged another part of me, which I did, and although she didn't actually touch me, it still felt quite nice wanking with her there and massaging my legs.

Eventually my hose spat out whatever it was that seemed to be tormenting it and once more I went out into the Soho streets. There is a feeling after ejaculation that puts you into an entirely different place to the one you were in before. Suddenly the street seemed to be remote and even a little unreal, vague. Just strange and busy people going about their heavy, laden tasks.

I passed the eaters in cafés in Old Compton Street and suddenly found myself tempted to wolf down a 'shwarma' in a pitta with some of that delicious looking purple cabbage which I stuffed inside until they dribbled over the side, and then I so happily crunched down on it, and was a little sad when it had gone and been reconstituted inside my intestine.

Having thus lunched I continued my usual pilgrimage across Charing Cross Road and then into Covent Garden. Here, for some mysterious reason, I always check the same shops and have never yet found the elusive thing I am looking for. And yet I continue to peep, peer, snoop, idle, examine, crave over items, like that black hoody in L.A. which was trimmed with silver metal studs down the sides and looked so pretty. But I did get the one with the crystals round the edges of the hood, and never did I feel so happy as when I had that damned thing on. And how I perved over it until I got it, until I won it, until I allowed myself the thrill, the sheer thrill of getting it!

And so, walking down that Ave called Melrose is to

submit yourself to temptations that might be unbearable, like the stores were full of sirens holding out in their bare white arms such delicious temptation, or like a magnet drawing the iron out of you. Until you feel leeched out, sucked and drained out, and almost slip sideways in where a lovely-bottomed young Israeli girl will sweet talk you into 'trying it on'.

— — —

CHAPTER 34

Ants of lust

──────

Of course it came back and there was a message saying 'I miss you' and by that time I was almost crawling with the ants of lust gnawing away at my vitals and so replied in kind, kind of hoping she might suggest an immediate meet. Which of course she did.

I did have a couple of invites that night, and so feebly making my excuses ... 'Go on take your time' as if in some way my wife guessed ... I opened the front door and almost felt the blast of freedom slap me in the face. Got in my nice little buggy and shot off and since it was a Sunday didn't have to worry about all that congestion shit.

Oh ho, slid easily into town and stopped off to get some pocket money at the hole in the wall, and soon I was there. The room was dumpy and dishevelled as ever and although she knows that we start on the grubby sofa she never thinks to clear it before I arrive and so while she was fiddling around I removed a few items like keys and a bag and bric-a-brac, and sat down, that is before I kind of lay down.

I was fancying her rotten, and so I lifted her skirt for a glance at her knickers which are always a bit spunkily sexy. And then she just climbed on top since I had my cock out, and my cock was not quite firm yet but enough for her to wriggle down. She removed her knickers and got to it, first the usual dabbing a bit of spit on my shaft since we never have foreplay. The foreplay is all in our minds before I get there. Since it was a hell of a time since I felt my cock wrapped in cunt and also thinking that I might never feel it again, it was a moment of sheer delirium. Just so delightfully delicious and she pumps away like a goodun while I just lay there and get 'banged'.

WAHOO!

It's got to last the night and so after a few dozen strokes or ups and downs she slowly pulls off and I wipe my cock, pull up my pants, and we get out, and this time to a quite pleasant Chinese which was situated round the corner and they had a cosy table and not too near a couple of rather loud big mouths sounding off. The food was marvellous and the evening passed in the usual pleasant sensation, in the knowledge there is to be more at the end of it, and that knowledge half-consciously stays in your mind like a backdrop, and provides just the slightest frisson and then we paid and left.

And soon we're at the scene of the crime once more

but this time we get right in to her grubby bed which always looks as if the sheets have never been changed but being dark blue they don't look actually dirty. So I just lay there while she went and pissed and then she was back and she slid on and was soon mounting my so very eager cock once more, and it was as delicious as it's been a long time. And it seems it was like this for both of us ... it felt like the nicest thing on earth and the closest you could get to infinite bliss. The she rolled off and sucked me for a while, while she had a wank. This is one of our most favourite things.

This went on for quite some time since she couldn't quite come as she had wanked only the day before thinking no doubt about my biggie and so she climbed aboard once again, and it was delicious as ever, if not more. After a while I climbed aboard her and it went in nicely and soon swelled up as it does when I'm on top and can feel suddenly quite affectionate and kiss her while fucking, and soon I can feel the gates open and before long I am squirting the thick hot spunky juice inside her.

It felt quite sensational, and one of the best it's ever been, and I slipped into the bathroom, washed my cock, put on my drawers and tried not to make it too obvious that I really am now simply dying to get on to the next set. No recriminations or begging to stay, just the usual, and I sipped some of the tea that had been made before our joust, kissed her goodbye and headed off.

God was I tired, but I was free of my lust and now could

continue to exist without pangs for some considerable time.

I hadn't seen her for a while which was very good and I breathed easily and was free with my partner and my lust was dormant, and so I was able to engage in all activities without that dreaded shadow lurking behind me like a slavering demon dog. Oh, the freedom was quite wonderful.

But then the bitch maybe sensing an itch within her started the messages which I healthily ignored for a while, but then felt I ought to at least acknowledge less the fiend got pissy.

I even did a couple of performances in a beautiful old theatre in Dalston and the shows went surprisingly well and the audiences cheered, the friends came, and I lived a normal life for a while. My technique was up to par and my memory was good, and the reaction of the audience to all my business was ecstatic and I started to feel like a man again. But then the itch, started, the ache started, the fantasies started, and my limp quiet cock grew stiff with thoughts that were naughty and juicy, and I began to dream of her knickers again. And lo and behold, I waited. Waited till my partner was out of sight, having gone to visit her ailing Dad.

And then I could feel free and abandoned, and so it was after a call that I was coming round and we would go for dinner and she agreed. But the journey was odious and I rang to say I would be a little late but she already had the foul smirk upon her and said,

"Maybe we should do it when you have more time!"

This was after I was half way there, and believe me, I felt just like turning round and ripping her dirty number out of my address book. But I said I wouldn't be long and she said,

"I don't just want to go to the café at the end of the road."

It was in fact a lovely café but she must have gone there with someone else, or made some trouble with them. And so we found a Spanish café off the High Street which we liked cause we could at least sit outside.

So we sat outside and I felt good for a few minutes to have found somewhere I could breathe in the summer air, and smoke, and so I ordered a wine and a tuna dish, which actually wasn't half bad, while her and her boy stuffed themselves with steaks since it was their opportunity to indulge and even ordered two desserts, which they couldn't finish. It would have been simpler to order just one and try it out, but her inordinate greed to (I repeat) make hay while the cock shines got the better of her, and isn't it always the case. Well, then the ugly bitch got into one of her rotten little streams about men as if she was an expert, which she probably is, of sour con men and cheats and low class trash. And what am I doing with all that muck, I wonder. And so she went on how Italian men are like this, and French men are like that, and how vile Italian men are, and how Jewish men are the best because they do as they're told. And I thought, not quite, you low sour bitch.

So the evening sped by with seamy dull chat, and I was just waiting and fiddled with her skirt under the table, and was getting horny in spite of the garbage being spewed, and then we left, and it was quite a lot with all their bloody extras. But when we got to her filthy dump, again we had to sit and watch moron TV until it was a respectable time for the child to go to bed, and I was getting really fed up, pissed off, and deadly bored. I think this feeling translated into my performance since although it was delicious at first, I bunged my load a bit quick and it was over, and I fled, fled with the greatest relief.

And then, there was space, light and most of all delicious freedom.

CHAPTER 35

Never stop needing

And so it seems to go on, and on, and on, and on, as we all crave our hit of spangly love. Our urges amplified mainly by the dearth of love in our past. Is that it? Is that why we keep needing and wanting and desiring and aching, even when the ache is hardly biologically there, and the need, the desperation really just a thin shadow of what it was?

And yet you crave it more and more, and can't think until the deed is done, like you were making a sacrifice, since we all basically need love so very much, and that love has to be proved and sucked and gurgled and drunk and screwed and sweated so that we know it's there for real. It's our link, our aging tissues coming together, and making out like young teenagers still receiving the sweet past when the world was young. Still craving so badly that which is fading so very fast, but don't let it go because that way lies death, and emptiness, and hopelessness, and purposelessness.

That's why we put up with anything. All the abuse, the sickening horrible messages, the loathsome accusations, the lies, the assaults on your sanctuary, since that sanctuary has to be smashed and you can't have it both ways, at least, not for ever. Oh yes, that would be nice, wouldn't it you

SELFISH, LAZY, GUTLESS SLOB.

That would be nice. Just to have a repository for spunk within spitting distance so to speak.

But you can't leave your sanctuary. At least not for a beast who is dangerous, and unreliable and capable of absolutely anything. Not for her. No, never, and when you did in the past, how awful, how painful it was, and that's when you wanted to break out and were going mad with grief and guilt. But no more of that and certainly not for this one. No, not for this one ever.

And why each time do I have to fall in love, and the worse they treat me the more beholden I become? The more I need them, the more I'm sucked into their remorseless labyrinth. And then you become weak and pitiful and apt to accept all manner of filthy abuse. So why do you do this to yourself?

Why do we become again like children craving, needing, begging for love, begging on our knees and when not begging, writing poems, plays, songs to our beloved. All weak and sickly.

WHY DO WE DO THIS?

What have we been so denied in the past that we are as adults one vast maw to suck in whatever we can? We need so much, and our need is a dependence on a drug that is stronger than any drug on earth, stronger than all other desires put together. Stronger than drugs, possessions, money, power. And how I used to almost leap when the phone would go and when on one of the many occasions that I had been swept away, when the plug had been pulled and I was given a reprieve, oh how I leapt into action. How I jetted round the fucking world for the bitches like a slave, like an addict craving a fix. Like an arm-punctured junky. And how many times you got off planes and she was there. And that became your world, and your new adventures, but then she pissed all over you.

But what adventures, what sizzling, delirious adventures like the time you were in a cab after you landed in some strange city, and you kissed her fat lipstick- smeared lips, and you kissed like there was nothing else in the world worth living for, and you even thought to yourself at that time that you would be happy now even to return. To get back on the plane and return. Because, nothing would be better, nothing would top that, seeing your lover, holding her in the taxi and sucking great wet oily kisses and if this was it, it would have been worth it. To sit in a cab and hold on tight, and suck down her cigarette-smoked kisses. And the rancid tobacco smell did not seem out of place with lipstick, cologne, powder, breath from the pit of the guts. And I would have been happy with that. Or maybe.

But of course that was your fantasy and you needed her so much, so very much, so intensely much. So much that you couldn't even fuck! You could not even

FUCK

since you got yourself so immersed in her glue. In her gluey, slithery soul you became a fly and yet you could no longer fly, you were stuck.

And then you wept, you sulked, became ill, became thin, became weak, became impotent, because in the end it became so very much, so very huge in your mind, that it became the world itself and the weight of it all toppled you, and down you fell with a great huge crash! And the drug had bit deep, deep into your bones and fibre and blood and soul.

But it passed and thank god for that, for you never believe that it will but yes, it does. Even if some tiny traces are left, some tiny cancerous cells that will be fortunately dormant unless you try to activate them again. Be wary, just be glad that you are out of the fiendish siren's grip.

But this one is no siren. Oh no, she dwells at the bottom of the swamp, where lay those creatures that lie in wait and then sneak out like sea eels that live between the clefts of rocks.

Maybe you saw yourself in her. Maybe you saw your match in her since she did all those wondrously, delicious things and was hot as a vampire is cold, and was careful and tender in her sex and so ... and so it's over ... at least for now.

And what was it but a constant reaching back, back to your own mother perhaps, to childhood, to abandoned love, and wishing always for this sweet feminine love, the soft, sweet, smooth love, and a love that you could never stop needing, never to the

END OF YOUR LIFE.

CHAPTER 36

An agent of the agency

A visit to the agent. A call to the agent. Apart from and separate from, and yet in some way connected to needing the bitch sometimes, like needing someone who has tripped up your heart is not too dissimilar to a call from your agent.

Of course it goes without saying that all actors need an agent and some need them more than others and need them to fulfil parental duties as if to make up for that lack of such an element in their youth. An agent is your ally, your new mum who believes in you and is concerned for you and watches over you and always makes an effort to come to see you when you work.

And there are the unfortunate lying scum agents who lie to you and deceive you and yet for some reason still keep you on their books since you might be useful to them, the ones that can't be bothered to return a call even when it is on a subject of vital importance, and once I had such a foul low-life agent like that. But that was in the past.

And for many actors the agent is a mysterious being, whose antennae hovers over the entire world where events are being put together in film, in theatre, in TV and like a water diviner he or she twitches when they get near the source, or the current of activity. They are privy to information that few actors know about and they even have the ear of those casting directors who are sought out and who have a direct connection to the heart of the film, the producers and director. Oh how important are these casting directors and one must never alienate them. For are they not the high priests receiving benediction from above?

Unfortunately actors by the very nature of their craft suspect that when the jobs are handed out they go to other dudes and that other members of the family are getting a bigger slice of the cake. And this suspicion would rumble around in your mind and the only way to curb the paranoia was to check in, just call in to check the form, just in case there was any news on the horizon. Of course any fool would tell you that if there was a sniff of an offer on the horizon you would have heard like a shot. So why ring, why give the appearance of a 'needy' actor, a snivelling beggar?

And, if they come to the phone, if they deigned to think you important enough to waste their valuable time on, you will only hear the same old bollocks

"You're up for a whole pile of stuff, John, yeah, a couple of movies will be casting next month and there are several good parts I'm putting you up for, yeah, oh yeah, some are cameos and I'm chatting to casting about you and they quite like the idea. They definitely like the idea, but you know in the end it's not up to them, but they're putting your name forward and you know, TV has gone down the toilet lately. Yeah, we did have a couple of availability checks on you the other day. No I don't tell you about each availability check unless they come through with at least a meeting. Don't like to tell you about each availability check. Unless of course you want me to. If you want me to I will, no problem, of course I can, if that's what you want I can tell you … sure, I understand … gives you a sense of how the market is … how it's going…what the

DEMAND

is … how your 'stock' is if you like, ha! ha! ha! No, no John I swear it's no problem and I can see where you're coming from. Sometimes it's good to know, I understand, gives you a sense of what's out there. Sure, we'll let you know John. Oh it's been a tough year, I kid you not but it's on the turn. The market's starting to buck up and I've got you up for some TV. As I said there's hardly any drama and more since those ponces or whoever runs the doss house called the Beeb have shaved it thinner than parmesan ha! ha! ha! But there is a big new series in the works and I'll keep you posted. Yeah, so right … yeah I hear you … you still doing those workshops of yours … oh that's great … that's a very smart thing to do … keeps you tuned up, keeps your motor running, smart thing to do, very smart. So be in touch ok? Oh, who called? Who checked you out? Wait a sec John ... oh yeah, that's right ... Eastenders ... Eastenders John, that's why I didn't tell you, no, no, I know it's the actor's graveyard ... sure, but if they come up with an offer I got to tell you right? Yeah, Eastenders, just an availability check. I know how you feel ha! ha! But I can't tell them to shove it up their arse, ha! ha! I can't tell them that, I have to tell you when they or anyone makes an offer, that's my job, that's an agent's job. But listen, they pay peanuts I know but they repeat all over the place and so it can put a few bob in your pocket. But listen I know how you feel so I'll never put you up for Eastenders. No, no, that's not for you. But if they come through with an offer you want me to just turn it down, ok? No? Oh, no? Ok, I'll pass it on to you if there's nothing better in the works. If there's nothing better and you want to put a few bob in your pocket, so I'll pass it on. Ok John ... Eastenders, definitely on the back burner ... ok John, gotta rush to find you work ha! ha! So keep in touch ... no John, no, it was just an availability check. I didn't turn it down, of I wouldn't do that without talking to you first, ok? Listen, we'll do lunch sometime, yeah that would be nice to catch up. Ooops, hey John, I've got a small army on hold, might be an offer ha! ha! So let me get to it. No! No! You didn't keep me, no John, you're important to me. Speak soon! Yeah, take care!" (hangs up)

SHIIIIIIT!

I wish I'd never rung him, why do I do it? It's like I'm asking him, 'Is my star still winking for me? Do I have an ally? Tell me please that I'm not alone … tell me … tell me that someone up there likes me … do I have a friend? Am I still connected to the universe? Am I? Right on the edge of the Milky Way but still there, still there.

Don't ring him again. Just don't. Have some self-control for fuck's sake. Horrible! I sounded like a beggar, like a poor wretched beggar with a dirty hand-out for some small change. All my life I've got my hand out, begging for something to do, to vindicate my existence. Fuck it… make your own existence! Make your own like you did once and it was magnificent. You hunted down your own beast, you brought down your own great dangerous beast, you didn't wait for some mouldy scraps to be thrown at you.

Fuck it … call up the workshop. I did. I called them up but only two could make it this weekend. The rest were busy.

"Gotta visit my sick mum on the weekends…"

"Gotta yoga retreat…"

"Working in a bar…"

"Going to a wedding…"

Blah! Blah! Blah! So I cancelled it. So, maybe I'll ring the bitch?! Yeah, maybe I'll do that …

MAYBE…

CHAPTER 37

The biter bit

Oh the horror, the filthy beast doth sometimes raise its vile, pale head just when I thought that I was free of the thing. Ah, what peace there is when that stinking vent is silent, when I am at contentment with my own lady and can frolic and walk around the town without ever having to worry about when I can get off to fulfil my wretched desires.

So it has been peace for a while since I couldn't give them the time of day. There is a kind of wholesome tranquillity in just being together and flowing together the way couples can, and in doing simple things like walking to the canal where they keep the boats and throwing old bread to the beautiful small ducks and relishing their intense appreciation of the crumbs and being disturbed by the small swift white gulls that dash in. But nobody cares, or no duck cares, but they continue to nibble where they can and that's so good.

I don't return her calls since I don't really want to

resume any contact with her, even when I have enjoyed it, and so has she, and we both had fun and good chats but the penalty for this, the price one has to pay, is so high in torment and grief and agitation and vile accusations, that one wishes it could only be all over for ever, and find something and someone else.

But now it's over and yet the beast still whimpers and murmurs and whines and always the messages are full of sly hints of gossip, or evil, and malice, and oh to be free of it forever. Please. It was fine while it lasted, those few sessions a year.

Work has been thin on the ground but we do carry on with the workshop when we can, and enough people want it. After several months of frustration and when I thought I could bear it no more I called some, and they were all surprisingly keen, and so I booked the hall and a few turned up. So we started work on a play I had been wanting to do for a long time and which had intrigued me. So we did. Our method was just to read a scene and then work on it and never ever discuss it in an abstract way but to actually do the bloody thing and discuss it only as we are doing it, and how what we are doing feeds into and amplifies the play.

Well to my utter astonishment it began to take on a life and we were all enjoying it and absorbing it into our bloodstream and feeding it. We worked in the old church hall in Islington, and this helped immensely, and a bloke called Mat brought in some very atmospheric music which of course the piece adopted. And it fed the play and became one with it, as if it had been composed for it.

And again I realised what a good bunch of people actors are since they only want to create, to play and express the most vital part of themselves. Which is in essence the best part of themselves, their vital spirit. And when do we have a chance of doing that? So we worked together for about four hours and we were all happy to be children again, angels again, birds flying through the wilder heavens of our imagination. Such sweet reasoning, such concern,

SUCH A DESIRE TO BE GOOD,

to do good, compared to the filthy bitches who love to hate us and abuse us, and not just us. Oh how nice to be simply a giver and not some dirty filthy scumbag who hides behind his or her column like a wretched spineless coward, so that they can bite with impunity. And how marvellous how wonderful not to be them. Thank god! And of course there are some good, well-meaning and enthusiastic critics, those whose enthusiasm has never worn out and who spread their enthusiasm and help us. And those we thank and we praise for enduring the endless round of junk, and yet are still able to rise to the occasion. But with our few gallant men and women, boys and girls, urchins and children, artists and mavericks, how hard they worked and how much they gave, since they were able to tap into that secret font deep inside themselves, and that's something we don't always have the opportunity of doing, at least not that often.

So we began, and I wanted them to move just ever so slowly since then we could see and absorb every part of their thought process, every nuance, every shade of emotion and when the whole group did this together it was just breathtakingly beautiful. Oh it was just so awesome for suddenly all their faces became transcended. They took on an image of holiness and so they moved slowly through space, this group of pained people in our Greek epic, and then the main character spoke, and how they listened, oh how they listened as if their very lives depended on it. As if the words would cauterise their wounds, as if the words would form a healing scar over their wounds, for that is how they listened, and it was beautiful to watch and each listened in their own way, each moved so gently in their own way and each movement overlapped with each other's movement like you might see branches in a tree as they wave with the wind.

And so, as they listened to the hero's beautiful voice ringing out they became like an orchestra, or like a ballet, or like some kind of dance since all were affected. Each in their own way and seldom had I seen something quite so beautiful. I also think that everyone felt it too.

Then we had a break and went a few doors down for a coffee and it was cold, it was in fact very cold, but I wanted a fag so I ordered a coffee, and went outside to roll my fag which I always like in the break, and then my coffee came and I put out the fag and sat with the 'hero' since I like sitting with him, and feeling the energy and sensing his struggles.

Then we decided to continue and so I went for a pee which I seem to do a lot when it's cold, and went back into the room and the guys were in good spirits and chatting and telling actorly stories, since actors always have stories as their lives are stories. And then we finished on a good and positive note and resolved to meet again as soon as possible, and not let time make a wider and wider gulf between us.

I drove home looking forward to my supper which I always do since my wife is such an excellent cook and I'm back early enough to have our precious child sit with us, which I like best of all since she can't stop nattering about what she did at school that day, and this takes away all responsibility from me since my guilt, my unadorned and treacherous guilt makes it more than difficult at times to communicate freely, and as freely as I would wish.

And even when I haven't seen the hag she still sends messages as if we were the best of friends and lovers and just can't wait to see each other. So I let this go, hoping that since I don't reply she will get fed up and cease, but to a lunatic who lives in her own world of fantasy my non-reply is no evidence as it would, or might be, in a semi-normal person. No, she just carries on with that horrid, awful greeting and why you might ask do I not just say, hey please just give it a rest, I don't really think we should communicate, let alone see each other? I have done this and there is peace for a while and then the disease once more starts to curdle in my lower nether regions and

FILTHY, SEXY, LURID IMAGES

begin to rise like gases from the depths of some sleeping volcano and then I am round there yet again. And so the horrible merry-go-round starts again.

But now it's over and has to be, since this person is far too dangerous as all sick people are. Having made this decision and embedded it inside my soul I felt better and soon the messages will fade and cease, and my soul can once more be free and unfettered.

So in my elevated mood, and happy to have once more corralled my splendid actors, and feeling purged, guilt free and enlightened, I swept into my street and opened the door.

I put the key in the lock and opened the door and I shut it swiftly again so as not to let the heat out too quickly. I noticed that no one was in the living room on the ground floor to my left, and the TV was not on, which was strange since our daughter is usually symbiotically linked to it after school and so I went downstairs to the basement area, down the small narrow staircase down which I have tripped so many times.

And to my surprise there was no sound of life, which to me meant cooking pots, chatter, laughter, the radio, plates, gossip, a small girl's voice. It was silent. Yes, it was silent, and this was a little strange but not too strange, since sometimes my wife goes next door for a chat with our nice neighbour, and now that my wife is suddenly into the performing arts it has opened the door to all sorts, an endless world of artistic endeavour and endless fascination, with all those sacred monsters, those wonderful brilliant demons that we can only admire at a distance and never hope to emulate.

So I went downstairs and into the kitchen which was now quite large since we had that extension made with sliding doors, and suddenly we felt as if we were living in luxury and I never ceased to feel an ever so slight thrill for years whenever I entered after the transformation took place.

And now there was the stove, replacing that horrible old gas fire, a cast iron stove, a black sturdy old fashioned beautifully made stove into which one fed little coal ingots or pieces of logs, and it was magnificent and gave out such warmth. And you could even heat a whole pot of stew on it which might take all day to cook, but when you got home it was the most lovely taste in the whole world.

Now downstairs, at the back of the corridor used to be a wretched old coal cupboard, a kind of dirty Victorian hovel for rats and insects and spiders and gloomy apparitions. So when I bought the wonderful Victorian house with all its sitting tenants, I converted the old cupboard into a splendid bathroom and that was my very own wonderful bathroom since the one on the ground floor had to be shared, believe it or not, with a couple of the old monsters upstairs, who never ceased to complain about everything and were a sad, poor couple from the pits of hell. He used to come in stone drunk after the pub, mumbling or yelling as his poor wife tried to get him up the stairs. On the rare occasion that I had to venture up there, the very rare occasion, the stench from their room was simply beyond belief. It was beyond what you could imagine any rotting humanoid could emit. It was a smell from the deepest pits of human misery. It was beyond ghastly but sometimes, yes, sometimes my poor darling last remaining, ever so fussy cat, might go up there when I was single, and if I was away for a night or two ... oh my poor beautiful, darling cat, she was a tortoiseshell.

But these sad people, this sad, tormented drab couple have long since vanished into the paler shades after a short sojourn in an old folks home and so has the batty old bird who lived beneath them. That's how I was able to afford the house since there could be no-one on this planet who would in their most wildest of nightmares even dare to live there. But I did. And that's why I could afford it.

One day a woman with whom I had experienced one of those mad critical, obsessive affairs where you lose all control of your body, soul and mind actually moved in. One weekend she just moved in, having had enough of dating and travelling backwards and forwards through London. One day she just turned up with two huge suitcases full of clothes and moved in and I of course welcomed it since someone was making a decision for both of us. So suddenly she was there and because she was trying to study the piano I converted my downstairs bathroom into a small office/music room where she could practice. I now had another bathroom on the ground floor since all the tenants had long gone ... oh bliss.

And so for a few months it was cosy, it was nice and blissful, and she went out to work in the morning and I liked that, and even breathed just the smallest sigh of relief when I saw her little 50cc scooter turn the corner of my drab suburban street.

However, as luck would have it she decided to fly off one day to America where she thought she might have a job, but the job somewhat depended on her being there and touting for it, and having meetings, and so after I had turned the flat upside down at least partly for her, she was off to other climes. She did come back for a little while but now her heart was there and so she flew off once more.

The one benefit of that was that I now had a lover in California. And how bad was that? And so every few weeks I would book a return flight economy class as cheaply as possible and arrive in the fantasy world of L.A. And so yes, how bad was that? That was amazing, even unbelievable, but it was always so sad when I had to pack my bags and go home. But one day I was determined to hang out for a while, like for two months, and that was quite wonderful. However she decided that she had had enough of all this to-ing and fro-ing and actually gave me the boot. They all seem to do this!

Now this caused me a whole heap of grief since I was such an obsessive idiot. Of course one of the side effects of possessiveness is being able to get in your clothes again which is no bad thing and I remember going on a kind of fast where I would eat nothing all day just smoke and drink tea, and then eat one glorious meal after my evening performance, since I was actually playing Hamlet at night, and my grief certainly lubricated the workings of poor Hamlet's grief.

So as I descended the stairs, the memories were swimming past me like I was striding through water, all surging past, every step of my descent, and of all the other hands that have gripped the banisters on the way down. All those hands, scores and even hundreds of hands. And now I'm in the kitchen and it's silent and there's no one there, and there's nothing on the stove, and the stove is cold. The room is empty and the cat has not been fed and is whining and circling his saucer.

But on the low table, the table where we sit and we eat, around which is a 'U' shaped unit made by my friend Alistair, on the table where so many hundreds of meals have been shared and millions of words have been spilled and gallons of wine had been drunk, on that table life had come to a halt. For on that table was a note. I picked it up; picked it up very carefully, as if its contents might be combustible, might explode in your face. It was a note from my dear wife:

'I can't go on like this anymore. I just can't. I know what you have been doing and who you've been seeing. This hag actually had the nerve to ring you here and

leave a disgusting message. It's eating me up and I have to go away for a while with our daughter. I can't say more for now. There's food in the fridge. I'll call in a few days ... Don't neglect to feed the cat!'

CHAPTER 38

Consequences

I froze. Froze in a kind of strange disbelief. Froze, although a thin sweat started to crawl down my forehead. The room not only looked empty now, it looked dead. Dead like nothing had ever lived in it. I searched in my pocket for my tobacco and took out the pouch, sat down and rolled a cigarette and took some deep drags. But the cat still whined and sat by his saucer so I took a tin of cat food and opened it and poured out half the contents on its plate which immediately the creature began to feed on hungrily.

She's no doubt gone to her mother's and so I'll ring there. I'll ring there but I'll give her a few moments. I just sat there finishing the roll up and contemplating an empty life, an empty future. I must get her back, must that was all.

MUST.

Why on earth had the horrible hag tried to destroy my life and home and sanctuary ... oh what a filthy beast! Why did she need to do such a thing, such a vile thing? Because her own life was such a chaos, such a disorder of the senses so she had to destroy mine, and all for a shag that I was too feeble to resist while knowing the consequences, while knowing that this was a possible scenario from a mad hag.

I knew that I had to deal with the hag once and for all. Once and for all, and for all time, since now this disease was creeping into not only my bones and tissue and plasma and blood and guts, but now had tipped over into my very sanctuary, my home. And for a man your home is not only your peace of mind, your sanctuary, but also your church, where you pray, where you make love and make life, where you rest, where you sleep, where you are ill and where others maybe ill, and where you also help them and aid them and soothe them. And where you dream together and plan together and talk together, and soothe each other's disturbances. This is where you can hide away, and not from fear, but to preserve who you are, and what you are, and where you plan and dream of conquering worlds and where you invite chosen and special people into your home to feed them and to listen to them.

And now the plague had entered my home, this precious chalice and had contaminated it and made it foul and the foulness had driven out all that was holy about my home. And so now it felt dead.

The cat finished its meal. I put my coat back on since I knew what I had to do, had in fact thought about it for some time, of what I might do if the worst happened, of what I might be forced to contemplate.

I climbed back up the stairs leaving the cat feeling bewildered since this is the time when he sees all of us, and jumps on the table when we eat together, and he joins us as one of the family, and I put some special treats for him on a little saucer. Not tinned food, but something a little different that has been specially cooked for him, like chicken breast or turkey, and while we eat so does he, for he is now part of the family. Sometimes a visitor is a little shocked to see the cat on the table but we just can't shoo him away since that is what he is used to, and will only jump on the table again. Cats in the wild always eat together and maybe he has this communal gene in him that needs to eat with us, and not just be a solitary being eating from a saucer on the floor. So just once a day he jumps on the table and eats with us, and we all enjoy eating together, for my wife is just such a good cook.

And now he looked bewildered and lonely and even confused. He looked like he knew it was a dead zone and didn't like it. He circled the room and jumped on the table as if he could will all of us back again. Will back the life that existed the night before. I thought I'd better leave the kitchen light on for the cat, and while doing that I switched the TV on, but at low volume, so at least there would be some of the things that made the kitchen familiar.

Then I jumped in the car and headed off, and I knew exactly where I was going, and though I wished it I could not stop myself. I drove the car to the end of our street, our simple suburban Victorian street which for years had been a neglected Islington slum, but was now showing signs of gentrification, where blinds replaced old tacky curtains and where walls were re-pointed and woodwork scraped and repainted, and much less dog shit on the pavement than there used to be.

So when I turned the corner I felt that there was no turning back, and soon I was at the lights. The first lights of the many I would have to pass until the eventual one. It was a dull drizzly typical London evening, and the small, drab British pubs were filling with their equally dreary occupants. Places I had visited in years gone by. Where I had walked and drunk the horrid beer and played bar billiards with others until the last ball pocketed, and then you'd have to put in yet another 50p for a further game. And why should I think of this now, of the little pub I used to visit with Annie in the early history of my sexual longings? Annie was simply gorgeous with long silky hair, and loved all the naughty things we did together and never was a threat. Never abused me. Never threatened me, but was always sweet and young and wholesome and even childlike.

Now I drove and was into Pentonville Road. That wide slightly sordid strip that reaches down to King's Cross. There used to be a nice Italian workman's café I used to visit on the right hand side, just after entering Pentonville

Road, and I got to know all the cafés since that is what I used to do. As a single man that is. Go to different cafés just to enjoy that first breakfast in the morning and so even if you weren't working, which I wasn't most of the time, at least the day would start well. Then a few more houses down there was the street that led into Chapel Street market that had surely been there for centuries and where each Sunday morning I would go with Annie, still Annie in my thoughts, and eat breakfast. At the little Italian café that was run by those cute Italian twins, and always I'd eat the same very unwholesome sausage roll with salad and we'd both sit and stare out of the window or maybe share the Sunday paper together.

But now the traffic lights again, and they were always red, always red as if they wish to forestall whatever event I had in my mind. To hold back. To wear me out. To cool down my mind. To make me rescind.

TO MAKE ME REACT.

I turned into the street which led to Mount Pleasant Post Office. And then turned right until King's Cross and more red lights, and the slow congealed bunch of traffic that always jams up before getting into Euston Road. Oh, the Post Office where I had worked many Xmas's ago when they took on more staff for the Christmas rush and how I had turned up and had to learn which towns were in which county, and did the test and passed, and then I was a postal worker and enjoyed being called 'comrade' by the regular communist staff when being told off. Like "Tea break is 15mins only, so don't take liberties comrade." But when he said 'comrade' there was no malice in the scolding. It was even pleasant. Well it was called Mount Pleasant Post Office after all.

And then I passed the large Georgian square where my beloved Alison lived for so many years in that ground floor room. How many times I would walk into the square knowing I was going to see my beloved and it made the walk that much more pleasurable. Poor beloved Alison, who sadly is no longer with us and yet it seemed minutes ago when I walked into the square just off the Pentonville Road.

So I drove, and as I drove for some weird reason the road seemed like a film that played back all the memories as the wheels turned, as the wheels turned on their way to their inevitable destination. As if the film needed to be played. As if it needed to be played in order to tell me something, in order to remind me of something. Oh god, I forgot, yes, as I turned into Pentonville the pub, that grotty, dirty typically British pub where once I rented the upstairs room to do my workshops and where I had tried to work on a Strindberg play but just couldn't get into it with the actress I'd been working with, who was a lunatic better known as Mad Maggie and who was prone to strange and bizarre outbursts of temper, like breakdowns, often accompanied by screams, shouts, accusations, finger pointing, abuse. And then she'd settle down only for it to start again. However, when she left I found a way of doing it. Yes, I found a way of doing it and maybe she helped since by shattering my peace of mind something broke through, and when I found the way, I became so excited, and then it flowed.

It flowed so well, first with Liz, and then later, the most perfect of them all, the beautiful and strange and elegant and refined Teresa. Oh, how beautiful, and what a sad loss as she too inhabits other realms.

And then the lights turned from amber to green and I was away down the Euston Road, past King's Cross and St Pancras, that magnificent edifice where so often I had taken the train to the northern regions. Where I came home, after my summer season in the Peak district, that so beautiful summer season when I was in the flow of youth and passion, and for months lived in the same town in the Peak district and never returned home but lived there in that same damp town where it always seemed to rain but the air was full of romantic young nymphs. Where the audience would clap at the beginning of the summer season to welcome the old lags back again and cheer on the new ones, and where you had a small dressing room and to preserve your vocal chords restricted yourself to one cigarette a day. And that only after the performance.

And of course wasn't it there that you met your beloved Jan whom you loved so much and made the sweetest love to, and how delicious was that after walking through the hills amidst the peat and heather to grab each other and squeeze the nectar out of each other. How divine was that.

But then it ended when the summer season ended and

I returned forlornly to St Pancras, and how crass London seemed after the sweet rolling hills of the Peak District. And Jan is with us no more, my beloved Jan. My sweet darling Jan.

The road widened. I shot up the great wide avenue of Euston Road and the memories eased up until I came to Baker Street. Just opposite Baker Street tube and a bit further down there were a series of narrow streets. Narrow Victorian streets with high houses, now mainly used for offices or nursing homes since it was close to Harley Street and the London Clinic. I would, like the slob I was, walk down one of those streets where I knew I might find my darling, sweet French au pair girl Yvette whom I had met crossing the Tottenham Court Road. Just met by chance, and then again in Trafalgar Square just passing through the Square.

It was summer and this lovely au pair girl was sitting on a bench and remembering me she came running up to me. She came running up to me and I could see it more vivid than ever before as if this was the last time I would be allowed to see it. She came running up to me and I can see it now, even now, and she was wearing her usual black pants and small black leather jacket over a white shirt, and how beautiful she looked and then we became friends and lovers for a long time.

And that's when I would descend the basement steps and knock at the window, no matter how late it was and it was usually after a night out at a jazz club and jive which I never took her to, since she couldn't have the faintest idea of what jive was. So after a night out I would descend the few stairs and knock at the window and soon the little light went on and her smiling face welcomed me, and she opened the window, since I had to climb in, the basement door being locked. And it was always that same pungent smell of a girl's bedroom with the odour of feminine unguents and creams and colognes and soap and it was always that same French smell. And I'd creep in and undress and crawl into bed and she'd make a coffee pot and then I'd spend most of the night tasting her since she was still a virgin, but she'd squeeze my cock at the same time so when I burst into bloom I'd stop and then go to sleep with my pet.

Now I passed that street and hit more lights. Red, red, and red again as if they were warning beacons, warning me,

WARNING ME TO STOP.

Think. But I drove on and on and the memories became thinner and more watery for there was nothing down here, nothing really of consequence, since I didn't lay down my scent down here like a dog.

And then it's Baker Street tube. I quite like Baker Street and all those years ago would take Liz to the Classic Cinema where they nearly always had great films on. Not like the shit you get today, but really great movies that you can recall for the rest of your life, films that lifted you up and penetrated your soul and to which you would take every new girlfriend to. And where you'd come out, heart expanded, moist eyes, heroic, in love with the hero. And it was at that time that I met Liz when working as a dish washer in Chelsea, and on that first night I took her back to my flat and shagged her and then we were friends ever since, or at least for a few years. And what was the film we saw that night? I believe it was 'Carrie' with Laurence Olivier whom I adored, revered, admired, worshipped as being the utmost paragon of what an actor should be. Or what even a man should be, since he was for me the perfect male.

RED. RED. RED. RED.

Why did the hag do that? Why? Why do women have such an innate desire to destroy your life, your peace of mind, just because you delivered a few shags on the side? But not just shags, for didn't I also listen to her problems and she did mine and share so many nice times and lovely dinners and occasional handouts when she needed it, and so why did she wish to contaminate my sanctuary as if this was the price that must be paid? How horrible was that, and would I ever do the same to her? Not in a thousand years and never have done, never, and there were times when the shoe was on the other foot. There were times when I shagged and gave succour to a married woman and would I ever even think of pestering her or calling her home or making life unbearable? Never, and not only never, but it would never even occur to me since that was the deal, and

I would know it from the start, and so why? Is it something deeply unbalanced within the female psyche, that needs to claim and possess, and that cannot even begin to share, and that resents the man's contentment with his home and family, believing that he does not deserve that? That the shag has a price that must be paid for, and a price that grows larger with each consequent shag until you are poisoned, and living in fear of exposure, living in fear of being blackmailed and fearing not to respond to her calls, less in her impatience, in her frustration, she calls your home and your wife, let alone all those other things that they are capable of. Even to violence. Even to that.

But the poison was the worst, the subtle and gradual seeping of her filth into the ears of others, through gossip, through messages, through nasty stories on the internet, and still like a drug addict I had forgiven and even come back for her and so the noose tightened until one day I did pluck up just a smallest vestige of courage and begged her, please give me some peace, a little silence. And this, this was the result.

And this was not the first time it's happened. For was there not another beast with whose womb I threshed and curdled my filthy lust, and was careless and let her know how I was sometimes frustrated. As all men are from time to time, and as are many women. And how she slowly strangled me, and yet I kept coming back, again and again. And the lust turned into a kind of morbid love.

BUT WAS IT REALLY LOVE?

Until I became a slave, a pathetic slave, and ran to her, rushed to her side, suffered unbelievable torments unto sickness while she caroused with others. But slowly, gradually, I was able to escape, slowly, slowly and painfully. Until the need faded and when I met this one I thought, oh god, at last a normal pleasant woman. Someone with whom to conduct a civilised affair of the loins, and so it was. So it was until the demands grew for time, for trips, for money, for commitment. And so it starts all over again. The beginning was simple and so sweet and so affectionate and so easy. But is it not always like that at the beginning?

I passed the dance school where I met my first divine wife and remembered the first meeting as you always do, when you end up marrying them. They seem to keep crossing your path. And I did some dance classes there since they gave special movement classes for actors and I went there. She was giving a class and she looked so cute in her black leotards and thick black hair tied back, and many times I went to that lovely old building which was a school for modern dance and therefore full of beautiful, healthy young dancers and I was proud to go there. Be part of it, since not so many actors could be bothered to do much more than learn lines and get pissed after, but not I. For I would be dedicated and work on my movements and my body, and a lot of fucking good it did me but it did make me feel better and be healthier than the drunken slobs who gathered each day at the famous actors' pub in the olden days, the Salisbury. And on the few times I went there I came out feeling foully abused by the booze, and soon stopped going there.

But by doing good, by trying to be better and trying to be good to my body, I met others who were trying be better people and doing good for their souls and their bodies. And so, therefore I met my beloved Rebecca, the beautiful American girl with the lovely voice and the high intelligence. That did last a few years. At least there was something to be proud of in my life. But that came to an end when I met some sexy dozey hag and was sucked into another abysmal turn of events.

Drive on, now near that street where I went to a massage parlour. A side street, Charlton Street, just off Euston Road, since in those old days my rancid uncontrolled brain would, when not engaged in the struggles of the soul, lazily slip down to my cock. And one day I noticed that sign, the sign that tempts men, and just went in. Never went back there again.

But then red again, and just past Eversholt Street and now, the first time in years, remember that hot summer when we rented a room there for our group having long left the one in Islington. It was a hot beautiful summer and we did our workshops there and by that time we were so much into what they called physical theatre and so everything was so physical, and summer in London is always so glorious, happy and carefree. In our break we supped on cappuccino at the local café and by then we had a really good group, fit and dedicated and how hard we worked and with such pride and invention. When one day we dared to show the results of our work how we were shot down by the critics, the bitches. But we never gave up. Never. We just licked our wounds and hoped that they may even like us the next time. And that was Eversholt Street. Near the horrid Euston Station.

And on and on past great Portland Street, and oh, the horror of the vile street for that was where I went to get a job. I was sixteen or thereabouts, and I remember it as if it were yesterday. I just walked into one of those warehouses that sell bolts of cloth and asked for a job. Any job, I said, since I was enthusiastic, and the man, the guvnor, gave me a job as a travelling salesman but didn't teach me anything about the cloth. Just gave me a load of pattern bunches and told me to get going round the dress manufacturers. And so I did. But I knew nothing about the quality or the content of what I was selling and so struggled and sweated and attempted to answer when I had not a clue but then I just disappeared from that vile and loathsome bastard's firm.

And what shall I do when I get there, although some shape of an idea had already formed in my mind, the merest shape, and its conclusion was violent. Violent to repay the violence doled out.

BY ALL OF THEM.

By all the bitches I had ever known and maybe this poor deluded and nasty cow will be the recipient of the total baggage that has accumulated over the years. All the vile baggage, all those fucking lies, deceit, tricks, needs, vanity, demands. Oh yes, the endless demands, the wants, the blackmail, the endless whinging of how much they have done for you, and what they have sacrificed, and what do I get, they bleat. Always the same thing as if there was something in their DNA. Something that must inevitably pop out, as if it was like a tumour, a tumour of mad insatiable greed…

The traffic was bad as if it was ganging up on me. As if it was holding me back, squeezing itself around me saying, no, no, no, don't go! But something was drawing me, the same way I was drawn almost against my will by my desire for the drug of her cunt, now I am drawn by the taste for revenge. Drawn, almost as if magnetised, and I can't get off, even though I want to. I can't seem to get off. No, I can't seem to get off the road.

And now the tape has less scenes on it for my activities didn't reach quite as far as this, although there were still some, still some faded grubby old memories of Marylebone, passing the filthy horrors of Edgware Road, that slimy stinking scar off Marble Arch that doesn't even seem to be part of London but now has become more colourful with tasty Lebanese eateries. But not when I was there as a young wretch in a filthy squalid menswear shop. Some canker in the middle of that dreadful road, a most repellent shop with the most disgusting leper of an owner who sat in the back of the shop like a diseased rat, and never had I seen such a piece of human degradation in my life.

But I needed the money and somehow I lasted there for three months, and don't know how on earth I did it. I should have been better as a beggar on the street. His ugly loathsome face is etched into my memory, plus his two sad pathetic excuses for humanity who also worked there. Uuuuugh!

So now I was crossing the flyover and floating above the damp relics of Victorian London and getting closer. Getting closer to my destination. My destiny. Closer and flying over London, then turning off and then I'm in the street, that over-familiar street called Hag Street.

I find a space and park my car, and yes, it's past 6.30 so nothing to pay. Out of the car and then my finger on the door button. Press, press hard, my nail white with the pressure. That funny electronic sound.

A voice: "What is it?"

"It's me."

"Wadyawant?"

"Just want to talk to you"

"Wotabout?"

"Wadyafink?"

"Nuffin to tell ya…"

"Whydyado it?"

"I didn't do nuffin."

"There was no need was there?"

"Wadyamean?"

"I mean there was no need to do wotyadid."

"Wadyamean there was no need? You wouldn't speak to me on the mobile."

"I was busy, you know that."

"Oh yeah! You're always busy."

"So why ring my home, drive the missus crazy?"

"'cause you wouldn't answer my calls."

"So you rang my home."

"'cause you wouldn't answer your mobe ... I had to talk to ya."

"What on earth did you say to her?"

"I just said 'Can I speak to John?'"

"That's all?"

"Yeah, that's all."

"And what she say?"

"She said, "Who wants him?""

"Wodyusay?"

"I said, "It's his lover..."

(Silence)

"Whydyado that?"

"Cause it's true and it's about time she knew. Cause you're deceiving both of us."

"Wot a terrible thing to say..."

"But it's true."

"Terrible..."

"But it's true. Better for her to know..."

"There was no need."

"No, no need for you, play both hands, convenient."

"So wot she say...?"

"Didn't she tellya?"

"No, she's gone, she's left..."

"Gone?"

"Yeah, she's gone."

"Wot, just walked out?"

"Yeah, gone, left me."

"Well now you're free. Arn't ya?"

"Free?"

"Yeah, you wanted to be free. Now you can stay nights."

"I wish you hadn't done that."

"Why? Now you can leave your mobe on."

"Why didyahave to do it?"

"But you're free. You don't have to be frightened anymore."

"It was horrible of you to do that…"

"So you do want to be free?"

"That's up to me to decide."

"You want to rush back home after a bunk up in case she gets suspicious?"

"Let me in."

"No."

"Why not?"

"Cause you'll hit me."

"Course I won't."

"I don't believe you."

"I said I won't."

"I think you've come to hurt me, cause you're hurt."

"Just want to talk…"

"Go home and think about it."

"Wanna see you."

"Why?"

"To talk about it."

"Why, nuffin to say."

"There is, lots to say."

"No there ain't ... nuffin ... not really."

"Have a cuppa and talk."

"You haven't come round to make love."

"Maybe, maybe yes..."

"Bollocks! You've come round to hurt me."

"No ... I'd like to make love..."

"Like fuck you would."

"Like fuck, I *would*!"

"Don't think so."

"Let's fuck and talk about it."

"Fuck off John or I'll call the police."

"Ok. Tell you wot. I won't come up."

"No you won't."

"So come down."

"What for?"

"We'll have a drink, have a chat."

"A drink?"

"Yeah, we'll go to the pub on the corner."

"Hate that pub."

"Alright, to the Italian café. They have a bar."

"Hate that place too."

"At least there's loads of people there."

"Just a drink then?"

"Yeah, I'm very depressed."

"You'll get over it."

"Maybe."

"And then you'll thank me."

"Yeah, maybe I will."

"You will, you'll be free."

"Miss my kid."

"You can still see her."

"Maybe."

"Course you can. She can't stop that."

"Let's have a drink then."

"I'm not sure."

"Oh for god's sake."

"You might attack me."

'Wot, in a crowded café?"

"You're mad, you can do anything."

"Just a glass of wine. Need to talk. Please."

"Ok, I've got to get ready."

"There's no need."

"Be five minutes."

"Ok."

Oh, doesn't she feel powerful now, doesn't she feel grand, that her poisonous mouth has pulled away the very foundations of my home, my life. The criminal female part of the mind that only wishes to destroy what may be your haven, your peace and sanctuary. In fact the whole basis for your existence. And now she feels powerful for there is, she thinks, nothing in her way. These human beings are merely props that hold up the sad male empire, and she has kicked them free and put us all in hell. Is the sexual act so powerful, so important, so earthy, that

YOU WOULD WANT TO SACRIFICE EVERYTHING FOR IT?

Men's crazy dicks that can only be appeased by the most inhuman sacrifice.

My mouth was dry and I needed a piss badly and wondered if I could sluice one off just to the side of the wall. The cold weather always makes me want to piss. I hopped from one foot to the other. And still I waited, fuck it! I pulled my track pants down enough to get my cock out and started but then the hall light came on, so after a few spurts I thrust it swiftly back, but then there was piss all over my pants making a bit of a dark wet stain. Shit. She opened the door, and thank god she didn't have that miserable git of a kid with her.

I wrapped my coat around me to hide the wet patch. She had the look of triumph with a bit of uncertainty thrown in, a little bit.

"So, where we goin', then?"

"I told you, to the Italian bar."

"Ok… you go ahead."

"What?"

"Just walk a bit ahead of me, cause I don't trust ya."

"Oh don't be silly."

"I'm not being silly, I know what you're capable of."

"What, you want me to walk ahead, like an Arab?"

"Yeah cause I'm nervous."

"Oh for god's sake."

"See? You're getting mad, now."

"I'll tell you what, go fuck yourself."

"I'm off."

She went to shut the door, but before she could, my foot kicked it open.

"I told you to get out, you're fuckin' mad, if you touch me I'll scream."

Her face was suddenly all pale, even yellowy, sickly and bloodless and I could see what a loathsome gutless coward she was. Like a rat that bites and runs back into its hole.

"You filthy diseased hag, all you were was a fuck to me. That's all. A fuck! And I couldn't wait to escape from your filthy hovel!

YOU SCUM!"

She was about to scream, when I seized hold of her throat. I seized her throat and all my power was directed into my two hands and she could only gurgle and splutter. And suddenly the lights went out as they were on a timer like a lot of those cheap lodging houses rented out by the Council. We were in the dark and she was gurgling. I couldn't see how she looked, but could only imagine. I could see the glare of car headlights through the small window over the door trace long white beams over the hallway ... I loosened my grip just slightly, but not too much, in case she screamed, but she didn't ... she was done for. She slowly slid down with a strange gasp ... better turn the light on ... she was dead. She looked horrible, white, and her eyes were bulging out of her head. What now? Let her be discovered ... they'll soon find me ... maybe I should call the police now ... no...

A relief her kid was out of course. He went to a boys club three nights a week.

I'll put her back upstairs in her hovel. And so I did ... she was so thin and light. I carried her up the one flight of stairs and then dropped her onto the dirty hall carpet and searched for her keys. Then I opened the door and dragged her inside and moved her into the living room area and sat her on the sofa. Her rabbit was scratching around. I suddenly felt a pang for the rabbit. Oh well, someone will look after it.

Her skirt had ridden up and revealed her knickers. She had the fancy ones on that she only wore if she thought there might be some nice sexy games. That bothered me. So, maybe she even thought that we might be having sex together. They were pretty knickers with a little ribbon tied round the top.

I suddenly felt sorry for her, for the sweet little games that women play, but this time she had gone too far.

TOO FAR.

She had tried and succeeded in shattering my life, in shitting over all what held me together, and so now I've shattered hers. For some reason her eyes had closed. Maybe with all the motion and tugging. In the madness of the moment I suddenly fancied her but that was only a chimera, a passing wisp at the memory of all the times she had sat in front of me with her legs apart — and what good legs she had — and how I had slowly wanked in front of her while she did the same, but not to conclusion, just as a warm up. We had such intimate times and actually we really got on until her madnesses came...

Must get out. Drive home and I'll phone the police from there. Yes that's what I'll do. I left the flat. Better leave the light on. Down the stairs, left the house and walked to my car. It was freezing cold but I was sweating. I got into the car and took out my roll ups and lit a cigarette, and sucked the smoke down deeply. That felt good ... very good.

BACK.

CHAPTER 39

Home

I started the car and headed down Kensington High Street, but there were no memories there except when I got to Hyde Park and remembered my youth. Remembered how I used to take the tube to Knightsbridge and run into the Park with such abandon and spend the day swimming in the Lido for nearly every hot day in the summer when out of work. I would go there and it was there that I met French Blanche, and there where I would frolic, and swim, and chatter to whoever, and the Park was my real sanctuary. Now I passed the Park and passed the Albert Hall, and then came to Knightsbridge, and somehow all these memories were vivid and in deep colours, as if I may never see them again.

And then I remembered the story. The story from the Greek myths when Paris had to choose between the three goddesses. Between Wisdom, Power and Beauty and he chose Beauty and abducted Helen. But I had not chosen beauty. I had always chosen sex. And that was the root of all my problems. I should have chosen wisdom or power and glory but instead I wallowed and with each wallowing I sunk lower and lower in the trough. It fulfilled a need that was deeper than any other need. It touched me as deep as my work, and even much deeper ... it seemed to have touched the wellspring of my being, the very source of who I was, it touched me in my most intimate part. It seemed to touch my very soul. But now it's over and there is a kind of sweet relief that it is...

Knightsbridge. Not much here except the memory of working in an antique shop that sold fake, or rather repro, 18th century French furniture, and was owned by a charming old poof from the north of England. Maybe Manchester. And he wore very elegant Edwardian style suits, and took me to dinner once at Scots of Piccadilly and I had never eaten so well in my life. But the job was deeply tedious and didn't last long. Along Piccadilly, where the brass used to hang out in the summer in the days when they could, in the days when brass seemed to be just about everywhere.

All the memories kept banging against me as if to say *take your last look*, but I don't want to kill myself. I don't want to, but for the life of me I can't think of anything else to do. Everything's gone. My parents long gone, and wife and child, and part-time slag whom in some funny way I might have loved since I couldn't let go of her. I couldn't seem to let go though I wanted to be rid of her forever but kept crawling back on my knees over glass shards.

And so now nothing ...

NOTHING.

People were walking swiftly through the chill night air full of expectation. Shaftesbury Ave and the crowds were gathering outside the theatre for some god awful musical that had been running for years but they were keen and full of eager anticipation since this was the West End and they'd see some rubbish and forget everything about it as soon as they left the theatre. They'd only remember that they went and had a programme as a souvenir. Holborn, then up Pentonville Road and it's beginning to rain, and I just want to get home, get home and feed the cat and have a long stiff drink. Then I'll call the police. And then they'll come and take me away. And then I won't have to do anything. I won't have to work, or be frustrated when I don't work, or look for actors, and struggle to put on a little fringe play in some squalid dump and be rejected by scumbag morons anymore. And won't that be a relief? Won't it just. And then it was the Angel, and how I liked that name. To live in the Angel which I suppose must have been a pub at one time and now the memories were flooding out of my brain like I was haemorrhaging them. They were seeping out of a wound in my brain. They were pouring out like they didn't want to be there anymore.

And I turned into Upper Street. Before I could drive, before I got my licence, I would always take the 38 bus or the 19. And I recalled a kind of bus inspector with great coat and a long bushy beard who used to just stand there and mark the arrival and departure of the big red buses, winter and summer, year after year, and it seemed to me that he tried to make this singularly unimportant role important. But it's only now that I realise that's he's gone. For some reason, only now.

Now the rain has decided to tumble down out of the sky as if the heavens were weeping for my pathetic state. A horrible state, a loathsome state and what's worst of all, worse than any of it, is the terrible loneliness. I could tell no one, speak to no one, and beg forgiveness of no one. And that was worst of all, the utter feeling of isolation, that there could be no one to comfort me. What a bitter lonely world this is.

As I turned into Essex Road, as I turned past Islington Green, when Islington was once a village and that was its green, and the rain was hitting the windscreen harder and the wiper was switched to faster, there was no one to talk to. Not even my actors. Not even them. And yet, how I loved them, and how well we worked together and chatted to each other after rehearsal and stopped for a pint but when it was over we seldom spoke, seldom met up. When we did it was ever so slightly self-conscious.

How could I beg them to please come and comfort me and sit with me in the pub for a farewell pint before I was carried off? Of course I couldn't and then I found the road I must turn down, and did so. The same boringly familiar road, and turned right into my road. Into my shabby Victorian row of houses that had not yet been gentrified since I had lived there. The less fashionable part of Islington.

The house was slightly lopsided which is why I was able to get it at a disgustingly cheap price apart from the sitting tenants who had now died off. The floor slanted ever so slightly as if the whole house was propped up by its neighbour. So I parked the car and noticed that I had left the house lights on. Noticed that I had gone out and left the lights on to be safe as a caution against burglars. I approached the house.

There was a great dog turd on the pavement just in front of the house, like even the neighbour's foul dog had contempt for me. I put the key in the lock and turned and pushed the door open but ... but something was different. The smell. There was a smell. A familiar smell. I shut the door. It was a smell of cooking. No, it's impossible. But yes. She was in the kitchen. Downstairs cooking. My wife was back! Oh god. I tumbled down the stairs and there she was. There she was in all her glory with our daughter and they both looked at me. I stood there. I just stood there and my eyes erupted and streams of tears waterfalled down my face. They just looked. Just looked. Just stared and could say nothing. But my wife, my darling wife bit her lip as if to hold the tears back.

"Welcome back" she said. "Welcome back."

But the tears kept coming, they kept coming…

"Don't", she said, "Don't, it's alright, I'm back, why shouldn't I be? Why shouldn't we be? Where else can we go?"

Oh god, oh god, it's too late, too late … "Please come in the other room. I have to tell you something."

"You have to tell me something?"

"Yes, come in the other room."

For some reason I couldn't take my eyes off the cat that was feeding hungrily at its saucer.

"There's no need, I know. I know what you're going to say."

"You know?"

"Quick come inside." Soon we were in the basement bedroom which led just off the kitchen.

"How do you mean you know?"

"Your mistress bitch told me everything."

"But … but no. Something terrible happened…"

"She let you think it had. She let you think that. She pretended so you would let go of her."

"She pretended?"

"Yes, she pretended. She thought you were going to kill her."

"When did she ring?"

"About half an hour ago."

"Oh my god, oh my god, oh my god!"

I collapsed onto the bed. I collapsed on my bed as if the world that was on the brink of being withdrawn from me had suddenly returned in all its multi coloured glory.

"But she left a message. She said 'Tell that bastard husband of yours never, ever to call me again. Never again. And if he does I call the police and have him put away', and 'how on earth do I put up with that slug of a man'. And I said, we all have our cross to bear and I'm truly sorry he hurt you and you won't be seeing him again ...ever."

She smiled at me, she smiled as if something had at last been resolved and she told me to stop crying for god's sake and wipe my eyes and don't forget to wash my hands and sit down for dinner cause they've been waiting for me, and so I did. I sat down in the basement kitchen and she cooked a simple gnocchi with the most exquisite sauce and some beautiful red wine I had bought at bargain price and I cannot remember anything ever tasting so wonderful.

And our daughter, seeing that somehow her father was at his most vulnerable, chose that moment to make her oft repeated request which up to now had been denied on various accounts, mostly to do with concern for her beautiful and vulnerable body.

"Dad, do you think I could have a bike for Xmas? You've been promising that for such a long time."

I had forgotten that it would be Xmas in less than a week. Everything had been erased from my mind. All joyous things eradicated. Yes, Xmas was coming in less than a week and it would be time to celebrate.

"Of course, of course, as long as you're extra specially careful, really, really careful, I will get you that bike."

"Oh thanks Daddy, thanks, and I will be extra specially careful!"

And she threw her arms around me and gave me a big hug and she smelt girlish and soapy. And I hugged her and as I did I looked up and my wife was looking at me, but as if from a thousand years away. And I looked back and thought that she had the most beautiful eyes, deep brown with specks of amber, and as she looked at me I knew that I could

NEVER, EVER LEAVE HER AGAIN.

STEVEN BERKOFF was born in Stepney, London. After studying drama and mime in London and Paris, he entered a series of repertory companies and in 1968 formed the London Theatre Group. His plays and adaptations have been performed in many countries and in many languages.

Berkoff's original stage plays include *East*, *West*, *Messiah: Scenes from a Crucifixion*, *The Secret Love Life of Ophelia*, *Decadence*, *Harry's Christmas*, *Massage*, *Acapulco* and *Brighton Beach Scumbags*. He has performed his trilogy of solo shows, *One Man*, *Shakespeare's Villains* and *Requiem for Ground Zero*, in venues all over the world.

Films Steven has acted in include *A Clockwork Orange*, *Barry Lyndon*, *Octopussy*, *Beverly Hills Cop*, *Rambo*, *Under the Cherry Moon*, *Absolute Beginners* and *The Krays*. He directed and co-starred with Joan Collins in the film version of his play *Decadence*. Two of his most recent roles were in David Fincher's version of *The Girl with the Dragon Tattoo*, and *The Tourist* with Angelina Jolie.

He has published a variety of books on the theatre such as the production journals *I am Hamlet*, *Meditations on Metamorphosis* and *Coriolanus in Deutschland*. Berkoff's work has led him to traverse the globe, and his love for travel is apparent in his book *Shopping in the Santa Monica Mall: The Journals of a Strolling Player*.

Urbane Publications is dedicated to
developing new author voices, and publishing
fiction and non-fiction that challenges, thrills and
fascinates.
From page-turning novels to innovative
reference books, our goal is to publish what
YOU want to read.

Find out more at
urbanepublications.com